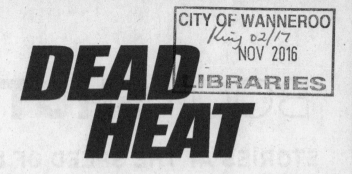

DEAD HEAT

JAMES PATTERSON is one of the best-known and biggest-selling writers of all time. His books have sold in excess of 325 million copies worldwide and he has been the most borrowed author in UK libraries for the past nine years in a row. He is the author of some of the most popular series of the past two decades – the Alex Cross, Women's Murder Club, Detective Michael Bennett and Private novels – and he has written many other number one bestsellers including romance novels and stand-alone thrillers.

James is passionate about encouraging children to read. Inspired by his own son who was a reluctant reader, he also writes a range of books for young readers including the Middle School, I Funny, Treasure Hunters, House of Robots, Confessions and Maximum Ride series. James is the proud sponsor of the World Book Day Award and has donated millions in grants to independent bookshops. He lives in Florida with his wife and son.

BOOK**SHOTS**

STORIES AT THE SPEED OF LIFE

What you are holding in your hands right now is no ordinary book, it's a BookShot.

BookShots are page-turning stories by James Patterson and other writers that can be read in one sitting.

Each and every one is fast-paced, 100% story-driven; a shot of pure entertainment guaranteed to satisfy.

Available as new, compact paperbacks, ebooks and audio, everywhere books are sold.

BookShots - the ultimate form of storytelling. From the ultimate storyteller.

DEAD HEAT

JAMES
PATTERSON
WITH *LEE STONE*

BOOK**SHOTS**

1 3 5 7 9 10 8 6 4 2

BookShots
20 Vauxhall Bridge Road
London SW1V 2SA

BookShots is part of the Penguin Random House
group of companies whose addresses can be found at
global.penguinrandomhouse.com

Penguin
Random House
UK

First published by BookShots in 2016

www.penguin.co.uk

A CIP catalogue record for this book is available
from the British Library.

ISBN 9781786530653

Typeset in Garamond Premier Pro 11/15.5 pt in
India by Thomson Digital Pvt Ltd, Noida Delhi

Printed and bound in Australia by Griffin Press

www.randomhouse.com.au
www.randomhouse.co.nz

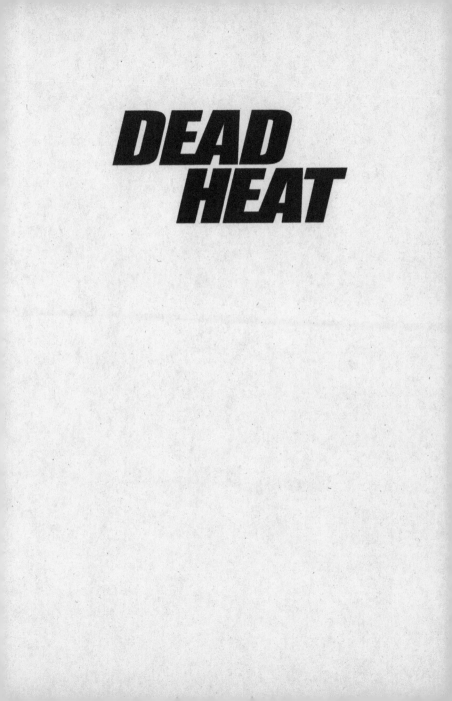

DEAD HEAT

PART 1

TIM GILMORE

CHAPTER 1

FOR THIRTY-NINE LONG YEARS, the telephone on Juliana's side of the bed has rung out in the middle of the night, the same way it is ringing right now. Juliana has never complained. Not one time. Whenever it happens, she just hands me the receiver, and tells me not to get myself killed.

The phone is on Juliana's side of the bed because there is nothing on my side except a wall. I earn a cop's wages, and we live in a house the size of a shoebox. I roll over and press the tiny button on my black plastic Casio and it lights up. 4 a.m.

'Carvalho?' Vitoria Paz, my partner for the past two years, is the voice on the end of the line.

I grunt. My bones hurt.

'I hate to wake you.'

'Everyone hates to wake me,' I tell her. 'That's why they always wake you first.'

I hear her sigh, but I know she's smiling.

'I'll be at your place in five minutes.'

She's talking out of the side of her mouth because she's smoking. She smokes a lot. Paz is twenty-six years old and tough as nails.

'What's the deal?' I ask, rolling out of bed.

'Missing person.'

I pull on socks in the dark. I'm an expert at this.

'Won't they still be missing after I've had a decent night's sleep?'

I hear Paz take another drag on her cigarette.

'The missing guy is an athlete,' she says. 'So you know how that goes at the moment.'

I know exactly how that goes. The Olympic Games officially open in a few hours' time, and the world's media are in Rio. Actually, the whole world is in Rio. And everyone, from the President down, is nervous.

'How long has this athlete been gone?'

'Twelve hours,' Paz says. 'Get some coffee down your neck – you sound irritable.'

I put the phone back on the beaten-up dresser as quietly as I can, but I hear Juliana stir.

'Rafael,' she says. 'Don't get yourself killed.'

I promise her that I won't, and I listen to her breathing soften. As Juliana slips back into her dreams, I use the blue backlight of the Casio to guide me out of the bedroom and down into the kitchen. I set the kettle on the stove and pull my badge and gun from the cupboard above the refrigerator. Soon Paz's headlights wash through the kitchen window and I get a first glimpse of myself in the mirror. I look crumpled. My hair is longer than it should be; still mostly brown, but greying at the temples. I haven't shaved for two days and I'm wearing yesterday's shirt. It's fair to say I've looked better.

Behind the wheel of her tiny Fiat, Paz looks fresh. The car reeks of smoke as I get in. It's warm out, and Paz is wearing a tight black vest and jeans. Paz runs three times a week, boxes at a local gym and benches one hundred and forty pounds. She hides her strength and grit behind a perfect white smile, sparkling brown eyes and a mop of black hair, which frames her face in tight spirals.

'Morning, Carvalho.'

'Morning. You okay?'

'Better than you, by the looks of things.'

I smile.

'That's not saying so much.'

Paz pulls slowly off the drive and doesn't hit the accelerator properly until we're out of earshot of Juliana. Paz swears like a bartender and smokes like a chimney, but whenever she is around my wife, she acts like an altar girl on her way to church. Soon enough, though, she puts her foot to the floor and I'm holding on to my scalding coffee with calloused fingers, hoping to Christ that she doesn't hit a pothole and scar me for life.

'Do you have to drive quite so fast? I'm two weeks off retirement and I'd like to get there alive, if it's all the same to you. It's a missing-person case, not a shootout.'

Paz smiles. She loves it when I'm grouchy. She has one hand on the wheel and is using the other to cram a new cigarette into her mouth, before flicking a steel Zippo to light it.

'The missing athlete is Tim Gilmore,' she says. 'Have you heard of him?'

'The Australian guy?'

I have an image of Tim Gilmore in my head. He's Australia's poster boy, and I've seen the pictures of him on billboards and adverts around the city. He's blond, tanned and tall.

'Javelin, right?'

Paz nods as the cigarette catches. Her eyes narrow against the smoke, making her look like a Mexican bandit scanning the horizon for trouble.

'Yeah. He's their team captain, too,' Paz says, taking another drag. 'Twenty-seven years old. It's his second Olympics. He's got a strong chance of a medal. At least he would, if anybody knew where he was.'

We pass rows of houses as the tiny Fiat speeds across the city. My free hand, the one that isn't holding the coffee, is holding on to the edge of the seat. The fabric has worn through over the years and exposed the foam underneath. There's a hole where Paz's five-year-old boy Felipe has been picking away at it with his tiny fingers. He's the only person who sits in Paz's passenger seat more often than me. Each time I get into her car, the hole in the foam is bigger.

'Felipe's like a moth in a wardrobe,' I tell her. 'This seat's going to disappear eventually.'

Paz doesn't bite.

'Gilmore trained late yesterday afternoon,' she says. 'But he never showed up to eat with his team in the evening. He's not answering his phone, either.'

'Late afternoon?' I push the blue backlight on my watch. 'That's only twelve hours ago.'

'I know,' Paz says as she winds down the window and flicks out her cigarette butt. 'Makes you wonder why they're so twitchy, doesn't it?'

'Get used to it,' I tell her. 'It's gonna be like the World Cup all over again. Everybody is going to be watching their backs and covering their behinds for the next two weeks, and if anything goes wrong they'll go ballistic.'

Suddenly Paz slams on the brakes and we come to a stop with a tyre screech loud enough to wake a city block. I look at her sideways as I swill down the last of my coffee and put the cup on the dashboard.

'Was that really necessary?'

'Nope,' she grins. 'But it felt good. Anyway, we're here.'

We park up on Rua Carioca, surrounded by thirty-one high-rise blocks full of the world's most talented athletes. Nearly four thousand flats. New coffee shops, flower shops and post offices have sprung up on every corner. But right now, everything is closed and deserted.

'Party central,' Paz says. 'Not.'

She is right. The air is still and the lights behind the thousands of windows are almost all turned off.

'Athletes love to sleep. It's one of the few things I have in common with them these days. Come on.'

Gilmore's coach is waiting for us in the lobby.

'Hunter Brown,' he says in a broad Aussie accent. He has a firm, dry handshake and bright, attentive eyes, just the right side of furtive.

'Carvalho,' I say. 'And this is Detective Paz.'

Vitoria shakes his hand.

'Has he shown up yet?'

Brown shakes his head. I frown as we walk over to a couple of sofas at the far side of the lobby. Hunter Brown looks away, composing his thoughts.

'I get it,' he says. 'You probably think I'm overreacting.'

I say nothing.

'Listen. Tim has trained for four years for this event. He wouldn't run out on us now. Not unless something is very wrong.'

He's genuinely worried.

'Has he ever gone missing before?' Paz asks.

Brown shakes his head.

'No way. We've been locked on this schedule for eighteen months. He calls me if he's heading out for a run. He calls me if he's thinking about eating something new. He's petrified of WADA.'

'The anti-doping guys?'

'Too right,' Brown says. 'They can knock on your door any time, demanding urine and blood.'

'Gilmore's clean, though?' Paz asks.

'You bet. But if you're not there when they show up, the world thinks you're a cheat for the rest of your career. Especially when you're as good as Tim.'

He sighs, and I wonder if he's slept at all.

'Can you get us into Gilmore's room?' I ask.

He nods.

'He's sharing with Oscar Ryan, the hammer-thrower. Have you heard of him?'

I shake my head.

'You will have, by the end of these Games,' Hunter Brown says and, for a moment, he smiles. 'Anyway, Oscar'll let us in.'

'Well,' Paz says. 'Let's go and wake him up.'

CHAPTER 2

THE LIFT IS TIGHT and intimate, and I get the feeling Hunter Brown wants to tell me something. Before he gets a chance, the doors open and we're out into a long, straight corridor. The place smells of fresh paint and new carpet.

We walk down the corridor until Brown stops outside a door and says, 'This is it.'

A brooding hulk of a guy opens the door and fills most of the frame. He looks as though he could crush a man without breaking a sweat, and without losing much sleep over it, either. I assume he's Oscar Ryan, but I never find out because he gives the slightest nod of recognition to Hunter Brown while scowling at all three of us, and then melts back into the darkness and disappears into his room.

'There's something you need to know about Tim Gilmore,' Brown says as he leads us through the gloom. 'He is not in a great place right now.'

The room is square, and one wall is taken up by a picture window, while another is covered with white high-gloss kitchen units. The floor is wooden and scuffs noisily, and there is a flat-screen TV stuck to one of the magnolia walls. A single bulb, underneath the extractor hood above the cooker, lights the entire scene. I fall into one of the sofas opposite the Aussie team coach. The dim light casts long shadows and gives his eyes a hooded and careworn appearance.

'What do you mean – "he's not in a great place"?'

Brown sighs.

'He has a media image as the all-Australian hero. He struggles to live up to it. This is the best chance he's had of winning Olympic gold.'

'He's feeling the pressure?'

'Too bloody right.'

Behind the coach, Paz is skulking around the place, picking up bottles of protein supplements and boxes of pasta. Looking for clues.

She stops pacing and sits down next to me on the sofa. I ask her if she's found anything interesting and she shakes her head.

'Gilmore's the messy one,' Brown says as I gaze across the unwashed plates and unfolded sports kit littering the room. There's a book on the sofa with its spine broken and a scrap of paper marking the point Gilmore had reached. I find myself wondering if he'll ever finish it.

Then I notice writing on the bookmark. I pull it out and turn it over in my fingers, before handing it to Paz. It's a phone number written on top of a supermarket receipt.

'Mobile phone,' Paz says. 'Could be something.'

'That's a local supermarket,' I say, 'so he's only recently written the number down. Who does he need to contact in Rio that isn't already on his phone?'

I pull out my own phone. I dial the number and listen to it ringing out.

CHAPTER 3

THE MARACANÃ STADIUM IS an imposing fortress, and there is excitement on the faces of everyone bustling past me, as I wait outside and soak up the atmosphere.

Officially I'm on duty tonight, supervising the VIP section. In reality, I have front-row seats for the show. It's a thank-you from the city for four decades of service. Juliana is holding my hand and I can feel the excitement pulsing through her. She's proud of me. She told me as much as she was straightening my jacket before we left. Paz is on my other arm clutching Felipe, her young boy, to her side.

'Keep your eyes open tonight,' she tells him. 'You'll still remember all of this when you're as old as Carvalho.'

Paz winks at me and flashes that toothpaste-advert smile. We've been working on the Gilmore case all day, without much joy, and we're both keen to shake off the day and enjoy ourselves. The air is crackling with anticipation and pride. The biggest show on earth has arrived in Rio. I think of Igor Morales, a friend of my dad's when he was alive, and now a lifelong friend of mine. We play dominoes together on Friday nights and he tells me stories of watching Uruguay winning the World Cup in 1950, with two hundred thousand people crammed inside the Maracanã Stadium.

'Hold on to Felipe,' I tell Paz. With every step we take towards the stadium, the crowd gets tighter.

'Way ahead of you.'

I grip Juliana's hand and push forward into the crowd. People are smiling and joking as they shuffle slowly forward. It takes us fifteen minutes to get into the VIP section. Felipe is wide-eyed with excitement. Our seats have been covered in sky-blue leather, in time for the Games, and cup-holders have been built into the armrests. I guess Igor Morales wouldn't recognise the place.

'Will you watch Felipe? I'm going to get drinks,' Paz shouts above the roar of the crowd, which seems close to fever pitch before the ceremony has even begun.

The stretched-plastic roof feels like canvas above us, as if the whole crowd is cocooned in a Bedouin tent as the last of the daylight begins to fade and the first of the stars emerge. Music pumps through the air, and the giant screens hanging from gantries high above our heads race through the superhuman achievements of previous competitors. It is visceral. And intoxicating. I turn and kiss Juliana's cheek, same as I've done for the past forty years, and feel the warmth of her skin.

'Break it up, lovebirds.' Paz smiles as she returns through the crowd. 'I got hot dogs.'

Suddenly the crowd erupts as, twenty yards to our right, the presidential party arrives. We are the *almost-VIPs* – the

security-approved buffer between the re████ ████ ███
seats. Felipe spots the President and poin███ ███████████

With perfect orchestration, the sta███ █████ █████ █████
instant the President takes her seat. Stars pe██ ██████ █████
through the yawning centre of the roof and the musi█ ██
replaced by the whistles of the crowd. Then silence. One last breath
before the madness.

When it happens, it is a roar and a cacophony. The first boom
of fireworks shakes the blood in my arteries, and there's an explosion of colour and fire. The music returns, driving and insistent.
Hundreds of musicians suddenly appear from every tunnelled
entrance and flood onto the arena surface, coming together to play
an ear-shattering fanfare. Juliana is inching forward to get the best
possible view. The entire sky is ablaze, and now, behind the musicians, hundreds of athletes are streaming into view. They move in
teams, bathed in restless and garish lights, swirling around the edge
of the field.

Flags start appearing on the screens. Afghanistan, Antigua and
Saudi Arabia all join the parade. As we watch, the Australian flag
flutters onto the giant screens and a section of green-and-gold-clad
spectators cheer far away behind us. The camera follows the flag
down to its bearer, a man in his mid-twenties with a square jaw,
broad shoulders and tight bronze skin. I stare at the huge screen,
transfixed and disbelieving, because the man holding the flag is
Tim Gilmore. His eyes have a far-away quality and he is wearing
earphones. He's chewing gum and staring straight ahead. I glance
over towards Paz, who looks confused.

at the hell?'

shrug and she frowns.

'Easiest missing-person case we've ever solved, I guess.'

I glance back up to the screen, but Gilmore has gone. Instinctively I move forward from my seat and push up against the waist-high metal bars separating us from the arena. An official heads towards me, but I show him my badge and he backs off. Instinct tells me to keep my badge out, chained around my neck, as I sense Paz on my shoulder. We search out the Australian team and, in the distance, I can see Gilmore leading them towards us in the parade. Fifty yards away, maybe. He is holding the flag in one hand, and in the other he has his javelin, symbolically held aloft as he leads his team forward.

'Is that even allowed?' Paz asks.

I shrug again, as my stomach starts to tighten slightly. As we watch, Gilmore hands his flag to a teammate. I can see that it's Oscar Ryan, the hammer-thrower. Gilmore turns and looks our way and, with his javelin held aloft, steps away from his team and begins to jog slowly against the flow of the parade, directly towards us.

Gilmore picks up pace, heading for the presidential party with his javelin held aloft. All at once, I am convinced something terrible is about to happen. I see his arm pull back into a throwing position, and finally the President and the crowd around her see the danger. Gilmore arches his back, ready to sling his javelin forward.

A woman next to me screams, but the music pumps on. Suddenly I'm aware of the gun in my hand and the cold metal of the trigger on my finger. I do not choose to fire; I don't make any conscious decision. It just happens. Three times, straight into the chest of Tim Gilmore. He twists and falls to the floor, and I watch a security team spill out from the VIP section and drag his lifeless body away out of sight. A huddle of nearby athletes watch on, horrified, but soon they are swept away in the tide of others. My gunshots were lost in the explosion of fireworks, and the TV cameras are pointing elsewhere. The show goes on.

'Jesus Christ!' Paz says, and I turn to find her right next to me, badge out and gun drawn. 'What the hell just happened?'

Oscar Ryan, the hammer-thrower, is walking against the tide of athletes and is staring straight at us. A tight scrum of security guards is moving the President away from the arena, but the parade continues and the fireworks still explode and the lights continue to flash. And the only thing that has changed in the world is that I've got a sinking feeling that Tim Gilmore is dead.

CHAPTER 4

ABOUT A MINUTE AFTER Tim Gilmore hits the floor, a group of Policia Militar arrive and bundle Paz and me towards the exit. Paz twists back in time to see Juliana grab hold of Felipe, and then falls into line with me and the boots and the berets, because there is no point fighting them. Nobody says anything until we are deep enough into the bowels of the Maracanã that the fireworks are no more than muffled thuds and the crowd is a distant memory.

'He's Tim Gilmore,' I say, looking at the tall military policeman leading the way.

He stops walking and turns round to face me, his eyes shining with a potent cocktail of machismo and adrenalin.

'He went missing yesterday,' I tell him. 'We've been investigating since five a.m. this morning.'

The tall commander inches closer to me and puts a rough hand on my chest.

'This is *my* stadium,' he says. 'My jurisdiction. And I didn't ask you to talk, old-timer.'

The commander is dressed for action, with his black protective vest over navy combat gear. He has a gun strapped to one thigh and another across his chest. None of it impresses me. I'm wondering whether Tim Gilmore is dead or alive, and this guy is worrying about the size of his jurisdiction. I ignore his guns and grandeur and look him in the eye.

'I don't need anyone's permission to speak.'

'You sure as hell need my permission to shoot in a restricted area,' he says, jutting his chin and getting in my face to emphasise the point. 'You're lucky we didn't fire back.'

He pushes at my chest to see if I'll yield. I don't. Instead, I slowly bring my hand up and take hold of his thumb. He is twenty years younger than me, but one of nature's laws says that if you bend a man's thumb back, he has only two options, regardless of how tough he is. Either he moves with the pressure, or he waits for the bone to snap. Moving with the pressure goes something like this: you move your wrist to compensate for the pressure on your thumb. Then you're forced to move your elbow to compensate for your wrist; your shoulder for your elbow; your hips for your shoulder; and eventually you're on the floor in front of all the men in your unit.

I see reality dawning in his eyes as he begins to yield to my pressure. Yielding to the *old-timer*. Our eyes are still locked when I sense the atmosphere change. A new team of tough guys break through the circle of men who are surrounding me and Paz. From within the new group the President emerges without breaking her stride. I let go of the commander's thumb and he turns to face her.

'Ma'am,' he says, his voice laced with authority and crackling with ambition.

She comes straight to the point.

'Who was the guy with the spear?'

'We don't know for sure.'

'His name is Tim Gilmore,' I say, and everybody turns and looks at me. 'He's the Australian team captain. He was reported missing overnight by his coach, and we have been actively looking for him since about five a.m. this morning. His coach was concerned because he's been suffering from some anxiety issues.'

'And who are you?' the President asks.

'He's the guy who shot the athlete,' the tall commander says. 'Don't worry, we're dealing with him.'

The President raises an eyebrow.

'You're *dealing* with him?'

'Ma'am, we have strict regulations that say we should shoot as a last resort. Two billion people around the world are watching on TV, and our protocols are designed to protect Brazil's image and reputation.'

The President shakes her head.

'Your protocols nearly had me skewered.'

She turns to me and takes hold of my hand.

'What's your name?'

'Carvalho.'

She turns away from me and holds my hand aloft, as if I'm Barão do Amazonas, the hero from classical legend, returning from Riachuelo. I'm not comfortable with it at all.

'This man is a hero,' she says. 'Anyone who treats him differently will answer to me, understand?'

She gives the commander a barbed look, before settling her gaze back on me.

'Can I do anything for you?'

'I want to know what happened to Tim Gilmore. He's a young man and he's trained his whole life to be here.'

The presidential eyebrow rises in anticipation as she waits for the commander to speak.

'Gilmore's dead.'

'There you go,' the President says. 'You did your job, Carvalho. And if you hadn't, then I would be dead right now. Whatever happened was his choice, not yours.'

Then she's gone. I feel sick to my stomach, thinking about Gilmore lying dead in some other corridor nearby, while most of the people outside have no idea what has happened. I've shot plenty of people, but this one certainly doesn't make me feel good.

'Get a statement from Oscar Ryan,' I tell the commander. 'He was right next to Gilmore. Find out what he said.'

The Policia Militar melt away without an apology and I am left facing Paz across the corridor.

'Come on,' she says in a low voice. 'Let's get home. At least we can beat the crowds.'

CHAPTER 5

'YOU JUST SAVED THE President from being killed,' Paz says as she drives us back across the city. 'That's pretty good work, Carvalho.'

In the night sky behind us, a million fireworks are exploding above the Maracanã. As Paz puts some distance between us and the burning sky, I can feel a familiar post-traumatic gloom beginning to settle.

'You can't kill a president with a javelin, in full view of a packed stadium,' I say. 'It's a hopeless plan. Doomed to failure. Tim Gilmore was on a suicide mission. He must have known that someone would shoot him. It just turned out to be me. The question is: why?'

My phone beeps and I look at the screen.

'It's from Juliana,' I tell Paz. 'One of the guys took her and Felipe back home.'

I breathe out and watch the streetlights pulsing rhythmically across the dashboard.

'Are you feeling alright, Carvalho? You want to stop for a beer or something?'

'No thanks, I'm all done with today.'

Paz says nothing for a long minute.

'You did what you had to do, Carvalho. You know that, right?'

I look across at her.

'It's easy to justify,' I tell her. 'Harder to live with.'

She drives another mile without saying a word. She grabs a box of Belmonts from the dashboard, pulls one out with her teeth and then offers me the pack, even though she knows I don't smoke.

'I'm fine.'

Paz looks across at me.

'Are you?'

Her voice is unusually soft, but before she can follow up, her phone bleeps. She shifts in her seat and pulls her phone from her back pocket. She holds it up and tries to read the text as she drives, and the car instantly veers towards the kerb.

'I hate it when you do that,' I tell her, and she shrugs, which is as close to an apology as I'm going to get. She hands me the phone and turns her eyes back on the road. She looks tired. It's been a long day.

'It's from Vivo Movel,' I tell her. 'Gilmore's phone records. He didn't call the number we found at the apartment, but he rang another athlete last night.'

Paz glances over impatiently.

'Lucas Meyer. A South African wrestler. Heard of him?'

Paz shakes her head.

'Do you think he was involved in trying to kill the President?'

'If Gilmore had told anyone what he was planning, they would have told him it was a hopeless idea. So no, I don't imagine Meyer was involved. He can wait until the morning.'

Paz rolls the Fiat to a halt on the kerb outside my house. Felipe is in the window waiting for her.

'You'd better be right,' Paz says. 'Because otherwise I'm going to be retiring at the same time as you.'

PART 2

LUCAS MEYER

CHAPTER 6

I'VE PLAYED FRIDAY-NIGHT DOMINOES with Igor Morales in the back room here at Casas Pedro for the past twenty years, and I have been meeting Vitoria Paz here since the day she became my partner. This morning the old bar is full of worn-out partygoers, and it smells of last night's beer. I take a coffee outside to a bright-red plastic chair that rocks on the uneven pavement when I sit.

The bar is hidden in the labyrinth of streets behind the Botafogo high-rises, and most of the drinkers here are Brazilians who know how to party. Some of the women still have green-and-gold paint streaked across their faces. The TV is showing pictures of the opening ceremony, and pictures of Tim Gilmore being dragged into an ambulance at the back of the Maracanã. It's not a great start to the day. I stir my coffee and mull over the events of the previous night. If I hadn't shot Gilmore, somebody else would have done the job. And if nobody else had done the job, the President would be dead.

None of it makes me feel any better.

I'm halfway down the coffee when Paz slips into the seat in front of me, the red plastic legs scraping their complaint on the rough pavement. Her dark complexion can't hide the rings under her eyes and she lets out a long sigh. She looks pretty much how I feel.

'Problem?'

She waves towards the bar, calling for coffee.

'Not especially,' she says, avoiding my eye.

'What is it?'

'You want the good news or the bad news?'

'Always start with the bad.'

Paz is about to speak when the barman arrives. She orders the same mud-thick coffee as me, then shifts back in her chair and runs a hand through her mop of spiralling hair.

'Captain's not too happy.'

I shrug. That's nothing new.

'He's getting a lot of heat.'

Despite the gloom, I laugh. I am genuinely surprised at his naivety.

'What the hell did he expect?'

Paz's coffee arrives and she flashes the barman her broad smile. He melts for a moment, before backing away and stumbling into a plastic chair. Paz's smile drops as she turns back to me.

'He says you'd be suspended right now, if it wasn't for the President stepping in.'

I fold my copy of *O Globo* and place my empty coffee cup on top of it. I'm seriously considering having a proper drink.

'What's the good news?'

Paz swilled the last of her espresso around her tiny cup.

'I know where to find Lucas Meyer.'

Half an hour later we're muscling through the crowds at the Carioca Arena, on our way to ask Lucas Meyer why Tim Gilmore phoned him the night before he died. The Carioca is a utopian dreamscape; everything is brand new and gleaming, and every pair of eyes is shining with excitement.

'Makes you proud, huh?' Paz says as we push along the concourse towards the stands. We pass thriving soda concessions and food stalls, and the noise of the crowd grows as we get to the hall itself. We emerge high in the stands, surrounded by thousands of fans. The arena floor is bright blue, and men are fighting inside bright-yellow competition rings. We head down the stairs. The closer we get to the wrestlers, the bigger and tougher they look. Paz puts a friendly hand on my back as we approach.

'Just like looking in the mirror, eh, Carvalho?'

I smile.

'Back in the day, Vitoria. Back in the day.'

I flash my badge and Paz flashes a smile, and a steward directs us underneath the grandstand to a cavernous warm-up area where the teams are preparing for each bout. The place smells of ointment and reminds me of my school locker room. Colossal men are stretching and grappling in every corner. There are no crowds, but the floor is covered with matting and the same circular fighting areas are drawn out in various colours. We find the South Africans in a huddle at the far side of the room and they break apart as we approach. There are six of them, three in Lycra and three in tracksuits. A man who is older than the others steps forward.

'Can I help you?'

His voice is rough, and his bulbous blue eyes bore into me. He's chewing gum at an alarming rate and I can trace the outline of his jugular, pulsing under his skin.

'Rafael Carvalho,' I say, holding up my badge again. 'And this is Detective Paz. We're looking for Lucas Meyer.'

The coach stops chewing for a moment.

'Me, too.'

He adjusts his stance and holds out a huge hand. It feels like sandpaper as I clasp it.

'I'm Aiden Nel,' he says. 'I'm sorry, I don't mean to be rude. I'm pretty stressed right now. Lucas is supposed to be on the mat in an hour and he's disappeared.'

Paz and I exchange glances. A loud slam echoes up towards the ceiling girders, as an athlete is thrown to the floor by a teammate.

'Disappeared since when, Mr Nel?' Paz asks.

Nel's bulging eyes flick to her and his brow furrows.

'He was at breakfast this morning. That was four hours ago.'

'How was he behaving at breakfast?'

Aiden Nel shrugged.

'Quiet. Watching the TV.'

The coach has lungs the size of oil drums and his voice is deep and rich. All the same, he sounds tight and pensive as he answers Paz's questions.

'Is that unusual? Don't people always get nervous before a big competition?'

'Not Lucas.'

As Paz asks the questions, I watch Aiden Nel's eyes drift slowly past her, and I follow his gaze. He's watching a girl heading towards the Russian team on the far side of the room. She's half the size of the wrestlers, with peroxide-blonde hair and a white tracksuit. She spots us looking at her and raises a delicate hand in greeting. By the time I look back, Aiden Nel's eyes are back on Paz.

'I supposed he was sleeping,' he says. 'Sleeping is a big part of our regime, so I wasn't worried.'

'But you're worried now?'

Nel glances nervously at his watch.

'He should have been here ninety minutes ago. He's not answering his phone and there was no answer when I banged on his door.'

I look at Aiden Nel's fists. I guess that most people would wake up if he hammered on their door.

'Does he have a room-mate?'

I remember Oscar Ryan glaring at us when we woke him up at Tim Gilmore's place, and make a mental note to check his witness statement when we get back to the precinct – assuming the Policia Militar took one, as I requested.

Nel shakes his huge head slowly.

'Lucas doesn't have a roomie. He's the kind of guy who needs a bit of space. I'm sure you know what I mean.'

He looks uncomfortable, as if he's betraying a confidence.

'Not really. Could you be more specific?'

'He has a temper. Life's a bit easier if we give him a place of his own.'

Paz's phone rings and she steps away from us to take the call. Behind her, the tiny blonde is making her way back across the room. Maybe Nel knows that I caught him staring before, because this time I get the impression he's making a point of keeping his eyes on me.

'Has Lucas ever gone missing before?' I ask.

'Nope.'

'Does the name Tim Gilmore mean anything to you?'

'He's the Australian guy, isn't he?'

I nod.

'The one who got shot.'

I nod again.

'Ever run into him?'

'Nope.'

'Did Lucas?'

'Not as far as I know.'

I check my ancient Casio. It's almost 11 a.m. I decide we'll head over to Meyer's apartment, once Paz finishes on the phone.

'One more thing,' I ask Nel, mostly to kill the time while I'm waiting for Paz to finish up. 'Did you notice what he was watching on the TV this morning?'

He rolls his shoulders and scrunches his face in thought.

'Same as the rest of us,' Nel says slowly. 'He was watching the news reports. The reports about Tim Gilmore.'

CHAPTER 7

IT TAKES US TEN minutes to walk the purpose-built route to Lucas Meyer's place. The sun is high in the sky and I'm sweating as we hurry towards the high-rise blocks.

'Who called you?'

'Vivo Movel,' Paz says. 'The mystery number in Tim Gilmore's apartment is an unregistered mobile. Untraceable.'

I'm disappointed, but not surprised.

Meyer's apartment block is pretty much identical to the one we visited yesterday morning. Inside, we find the building supervisor. He looks leathery, with curled nails and yellow teeth. He's wearing a smart shirt, but his hands are gnarled and scarred, and I wonder what he did for a living before the Olympics rolled into town.

'We need to get into Lucas Meyer's room,' I tell him. 'He's not opening up.'

I'm expecting the supervisor to have a weighty bunch of keys, but instead he pulls out a single plastic card.

'Access all areas,' he says with a toothy grin.

The world has changed, and I can feel my retirement looming.

We take the lift to the thirteenth floor, and the doors open onto a corridor just like the one Tim Gilmore was living on. Lucas Meyer's front door is identical, too. I don't like the feeling of déjà vu.

'Television,' the supervisor says, as we hear the burbling noise from behind Meyer's door. Pleased at his own helpfulness, he exposes his yellow teeth again. Paz bangs hard on the door and, when there's no response, she kicks at it hard enough to bring Meyer's neighbour out into the corridor. A tall, bleary-eyed man in his mid-twenties leans around his door and asks us what's going on.

'Police business,' Paz says. 'Go back inside.'

The neighbour is twelve inches taller than Paz, but Paz is in full flow. Her eyes are a mix of adrenalin and authority, and the athlete does exactly what he's told.

We wait. I hear no movement behind Meyer's door, and nobody opens it up. I turn to the supervisor, who pre-empts my request and leans in to swipe his card. I catch a smell of rot on his breath, and suddenly his teeth remind me of the seeds from an overripe melon. I have a primal urge to keep him at arm's length.

'Stay here,' I tell him, as Paz and I sweep inside. There's a short, dark corridor from the front door to the lounge, tight enough that we need to walk in single file. An alcove on the left leads to a kitchenette. There's nothing on the stove, and a single mug is draining near the sink. I pull open the nearest cupboard. It's packed with pasta and rice. There are eggs and meat in the humming refrigerator.

'Hungry guy,' Paz mutters, joining me in the doorway. 'Nothing in the bathroom, by the way.'

As we push further along the corridor, I'm vaguely aware of the supervisor's rotten breath and I realise he's ignored my instructions to wait outside. Paz pushes through the door at the end of the short corridor and moves slowly into the lounge. The blinds are drawn and the room is dark, except for the television that is sending flickering shadows against the far wall. Nobody is watching. I look at Paz, who looks back at me and shrugs. The television is uncomfortably loud, making it hard to think straight. I can't find the remote and eventually pull the plug out of the wall. Paz takes a minute to breathe.

'Okay,' she says. 'That's better. So where is he?'

Sometimes you can feel the bad news coming.

'He's here, somewhere.'

Paz nods as the silence begins to settle.

'Well, there's only the bedroom left.'

She walks out into the corridor and straight into the supervisor, who is lurking in the gloom.

'Jesus Christ,' she says. 'Can you wait outside, please?'

I take the lead and push into the bedroom. The blinds are wide open, and bright daylight streams in from the opening doorway. As my pupils adjust, I begin to make out the geography. There is a large, neatly made bed in the centre and beyond it a window framing the beautiful interlocking stadia of the Barra da Tijuca Olympic Park. Silhouetted in the window is the giant frame of a colossal man. He is sitting on the floor with his back to us, leaning against the bed. He has the thickest neck of any person I have ever seen in my life. His light hair is tightly cropped, and he's wearing a plain grey T-shirt stretched over huge slabs of muscle. What I can't see is his face.

'Lucas Meyer?'

No response.

Paz moves into the room beside me and draws her gun, on instinct. She covers me as I step forward. I move around the bed, slowly bringing myself into Meyer's line of sight. I see his fingertips first. They're blue. As I walk around in front of him, I spot the pill bottle that he is still clutching. I prise it from his cold fingers and hand it to Paz, who is already holstering her weapon.

'Overdose,' I say. 'What are they?'

She checks the label, as I check without much hope for a pulse in Meyer's huge neck. I feel nothing. His skin is cold and clammy and his dull eyes are still open. It feels like he's staring at me as I go about my grim task. His face is pallid and his lips are blue. His head has lolled slightly to one side, and an elastic thread of drool is hanging from the corner of his mouth.

Paz looks up from the bottle.

'Sleeping pills. Zopiclone.'

As Paz begins reading through the ingredients, I notice vomit covering Meyer's grey T-shirt and the legs of his jeans. It's enough to make me lean in and check his pulse again, because much of what he's swallowed hasn't made it into his system. I thrust two fingers as hard as I can into his neck. It's like trying to get a pulse out of a rhino. I hold my breath, and after a few seconds I look up at Paz.

'Call an ambulance,' I tell her. 'He's still alive.'

CHAPTER 8

PAZ IS TAILGATING THE ambulance as it speeds along the Linha Amarela towards the emergency room at the Hospital Federal de Bonsucesso.

'Think you did enough?' she asks as we plough through another set of red lights. I am drenched with sweat, after pumping Meyer's massive chest for fifteen minutes while we waited for the ambulance to arrive.

'I don't know. It's pretty difficult to kill yourself with modern sleeping pills. The lethality has been designed out of them. Especially if you're the size of Lucas Meyer. And especially if your body has ejected half of what you swallowed. But if he pulls through, I'm not sure we'll have done him any favours.'

Paz steals a glance at me.

'Why not?'

'His fingers were blue, Paz. The lack of oxygen will have ruined his brain, and the Zopiclone will have ruined his liver. If he lives, he'll never wrestle again. He'll probably never speak again.'

The ambulance hits a pothole, and Paz swerves to avoid doing the same.

'That's a pity,' she says. 'I've got a stack of questions I'd like to ask him.'

It takes fifteen minutes to reach the hospital, and another three to negotiate the swarm of white minibuses and the badly parked cars. Paz flashes her badge and we're waved through the security checkpoint in time to see Meyer being pulled from the back of the ambulance. They're still working on him as they wheel him into the building. Inside, we wait five minutes until a man in a smart shirt with rolled-up sleeves finds us in the waiting area.

'Dr Pereyra,' he says as he approaches.

'Detectives Carvalho and Paz,' I tell him. 'Is he going to pull through?'

Pereyra shows me the palms of his hands and rounds his shoulders, as if the weight of the world is on his back.

'Maybe. He's responding to treatment, but some of his organs may have shut down completely. And there's a strong possibility of brain damage.'

Once Pereyra has gone, Paz grabs two polystyrene cups of coffee from an ancient vending machine. We sit down and get our heads together over a chipped Formica coffee table. We talk quietly, the way anxious relatives discuss the best and worst scenarios while they wait for news to reach them.

'Here's what we know,' Paz says. 'Two nights ago, Gilmore phones Meyer. Gilmore disappears. Last night he reappears, attempts to throw a javelin at the President and you shoot him.'

I wince at the memory.

'This morning Meyer watches the news reports about Gilmore at breakfast, and we find him in his room having swallowed enough sedatives to knock out an elephant. Coincidence?'

I shake my head.

'No chance.' I take a sip of my coffee and scald my top lip.

'Why set the machine so hot?' I complain. Paz watches me over the rim of her cup as she blows to cool her own drink. 'One thing's for sure: Lucas Meyer knows something. He spoke to Gilmore before the attack, and he tried to kill himself after.'

'Meyer's not going to be talking any time soon,' Paz says.

'True. But it means there's something worth knowing. We just need to find out what it is.'

A receptionist calls out to us across the lobby. Paz and I turn to see a nervous-looking woman holding two fingers in the air.

'Excuse me?' she says, beckoning us towards her. We walk closer and she lowers her voice. She puts the hand that was in the air over the mouthpiece of her telephone. 'Are you the police?'

I nod.

'Here about Lucas Meyer?'

I nod again and show her my badge.

'Someone on the phone is asking for him,' she almost whispers. 'What should I say?'

I take the phone from her and hold it to my ear. No background noise. No clues.

'Hello?' I say.

The voice on the line says, 'Who's that?'

'You first.'

There's a pause.

'My name is Dr Rahim Jaffari. I am Lucas Meyer's psychologist. I insist on speaking with him. Are you a doctor?'

He sounds suave and sophisticated. His Middle Eastern accent is rich and complex in tone.

'No. I'm Detective Rafael Carvalho. Can we talk?'

Paz watches me intently, trying to guess what I am hearing on the line.

'Talk about what?'

'Lucas has swallowed half a bottle of sleeping pills.'

'Okay,' Jaffari says. 'Well, I didn't prescribe them.'

'I'm not suggesting you did. But if he's your client, maybe you can tell me something about his state of mind?'

'I never discuss my clients.'

His tone is uncompromising.

'I'd hate to have to arrest you.'

Jaffari laughs.

'You're a very persuasive man, Detective Carvalho.'

'This is not a game,' I tell him. 'Your client tried to take his own life. If you know why, you need to tell me.'

He adjusts his tone to something more conciliatory.

'It's not a game to me, either,' he says. 'But you have to understand that I provide very private assistance to very public people. What they tell me is confidential.'

I clear my throat.

'There's a good chance Lucas Meyer is going to die.'

There's a pause as the psychologist assesses his position.

'Okay, I'll talk to you,' he says after a minute. 'But not over the phone.'

CHAPTER 9

BY THE TIME WE arrive at the Belmond Copacabana Palace, Rahim Jaffari is already taking lunch on the terrace next to a shimmering pool. The hotel is a white Art Deco block, with the name wrought in huge copper letters above the sixth-floor windows.

'Dr Jaffari?'

Jaffari smiles and invites me to sit. He's a good-looking man in his mid-fifties. He has olive skin that retains a youthful quality and striking white hair that is fashionably cut.

'Detective Carvalho,' he says. 'Thank you for coming.'

I introduce Paz, and Jaffari nods politely. His smile vanishes as we sit, and I figure he wants to get down to business. The table, which overlooks the Guanabara Bay, is covered with a crisp white cotton tablecloth and furnished with fine china plates. A prim waitress stands nearby, wearing a crisp white shirt and a patterned sarong. Jaffari beckons her over and asks her to bring a fresh pot of coffee.

'Can you imagine competing in this heat?' he asks, watching the waitress swish off in her sarong. I say nothing. I don't know exactly what Jaffari can tell me, but I haven't come here to talk about the weather. Jaffari is comfortable with the silence, and for a while we both stare out towards the horizon, our eyes narrowed slightly against the breeze coming in off the water. After a moment, the coffee arrives.

'What is it that you could not tell me over the phone?' I ask Jaffari as he pours.

'It's difficult.'

'I figured as much. You didn't want to talk to me at all, earlier.'

I sip the coffee. It tastes a world better than the stuff from the vending machine in the hospital. Jaffari sighs and takes a moment to rearrange the cutlery until it is perfectly symmetrical.

'Lucas Meyer is my client,' he says slowly. 'I owe him my confidentiality.'

I look back from the sea and stare at him.

'This is not the time for secrets. I've got one athlete in hospital and another in the morgue.'

'It wasn't me who shot him,' Jaffari says bluntly, and for a second I think I see a smile play on the corners of his lips.

Paz puts her cup down a little harder than she intended and the spoon rattles on the china saucer.

'You have to understand that my clients only come to me in secret,' Jaffari continues. 'Publically I won't admit to even knowing my patients, let alone revealing what we've worked on together. If I speak to you, my reputation will be ruined.'

I resist the urge to tell him that two lives have been ruined in the past twenty-four hours, and that I don't give a damn about his career.

'Dr Jaffari, I assure you this is a privileged conversation. But I am investigating the death of Tim Gilmore and the attempted suicide of your client, and I need to know what you can tell me.'

The breeze whips up one corner of the white tablecloth and topples a wine glass towards the floor. On impulse, my hand springs forward and catches it. I smooth down the tablecloth and put the glass back on top. I'm two weeks away from retirement, but there's nothing wrong with my reflexes.

'Last year I had a call from a guy called Aiden Nel,' Jaffari says. I look up, remembering the man with the sandpaper-handshake who met us backstage at the Carioca Arena. 'Meyer's coach. He was worried about one of his athletes. He tells me Meyer is struggling with the pressure, ahead of the Olympics.'

'It's the biggest moment of an athlete's life. It's bound to come with pressure.'

'Maybe,' Jaffari says. 'But you have to understand that pressure is like a button, or a switch that can be turned on or off. You think you've got it under control, and then suddenly it can change. Sometimes you don't realise you're losing control of it until the button is pressed and you do something... *spectacular*. It can happen in any walk of life. Not just sport.'

His tone is patronising.

'So why did Aiden Nel call you? Had Meyer's button been pressed?'

I try to keep the sarcasm out of my voice.

'Coaches come to me with all sorts of issues. Athletes who need to find an edge somewhere. Better focus in training, more aggression in competition – that kind of thing. Sometimes they're suffering from a problem. Drugs. Addiction. Anger issues. Sexual deviances. Gambling. You name it.'

'What about Meyer?'

'Meyer couldn't cope with the media schedule, the sponsor meetings and the photo shoots. He's wasn't that kind of guy. So Aiden Nel wanted my help.'

Jaffari looks back out to the horizon.

'The coach told me he was worried about how Meyer was acting. He said Meyer had anger issues and personality problems.'

For a second time I remember Oscar Ryan, and the glowering way he looked at me in the Maracanã after I had shot Gilmore. Ryan was another athlete with anger issues, but according to Paz, his statement checked out. Oscar Ryan was a dead end.

'The coach arranged for Lucas to take a holiday for a fortnight. I just happened to take a holiday at the same time. In the same hotel. And we met up. Every day.'

'Is that how it works?' I ask.

'Sometimes.'

I imagine Meyer and Jaffari sitting at a table like this, in the sunshine near a pool.

'Where?'

Jaffari looks at me. In the sunlight, his brown eyes look almost amber, calm and calculating.

'Does it matter?'

I shrug. I guess it probably doesn't.

'Nairobi,' Jaffari says after a minute. 'In Kenya. I met him halfway.'

In my mind, I calculate the distance between Johannesburg and Nairobi, and begin to wonder where Jaffari himself might have been flying from. I decide not to ask. I have other, more pressing questions and Jaffari looks like he could clam up at any time he liked.

'We met every day and processed some of the things that were bothering him. He just wanted to be the best in his field.'

'I thought he *was* the best?'

Jaffari smiles wryly.

'The human animal is not programmed to be satisfied,' he says. 'I bet you celebrated becoming a detective, back in the day, but you've probably spent the past few years asking yourself why you never made Chief, right?'

He studies my reaction with his amber eyes, as if I'm one of his clients.

'Too late to worry about that now,' I tell him tersely, and flash him an acerbic smile.

'My point is that people are never satisfied. Neither is Meyer. Paupers spend their lives wanting to be princes, and princes spend their lives waiting to be kings. And once they're kings, they want to expand their empires. We're all human. It's what we do. Lucas Meyer is no different.'

'In what way?'

'He wants to be the best ever. He wants to be remembered for a thousand years. The media and the photo shoots are all distractions to him.'

'Distractions that were causing the moods and the anxiety?'

Jaffari leans forward very slightly.

'Partly,' he says, as the breeze picks up over the Guanabara Bay and ripples the calm turquoise of the pool. 'Meyer told me he was dependent on drugs.'

Jaffari leans back, unburdened.

'What kind of drugs?'

The psychologist pauses, calculating.

'You understand that under normal circumstances I would not be able to tell you about this?'

Under normal circumstances, I'd throw you in a cell, I think.

I repeat the question. Jaffari shifts in his chair and rolls his shoulders back.

'Performance-enhancing,' he says. 'Apparently undetectable. Meyer's supplier was a step ahead of the testers.'

'Did he tell you who was supplying?'

'Of course not. By the time he realised the drugs were causing anxiety and rage, he was hooked. He began to believe that, before Rio, WADA would find a test to detect whatever he was taking. He became obsessed with the idea that he was going to be caught and that he'd ruin his legacy. He was terrified. The closer he got to the Games, the higher the stakes rose and the more paranoid he became.'

I watch the blurred horizon, the sea washing into the cloudless sky. I think about Meyer, a colossal man reduced to a paranoid wreck, downing pills to end his misery. Jaffari's theory is possible. Across the table, Paz catches my eye and I remember she's due to pick up Felipe from school. I get the feeling Jaffari has spilt as much as he's prepared to share anyway. I thank him for his time and we walk back through the hotel lobby, feeling that we're leaving with more questions than answers.

We are both quiet as I ride with Paz to Felipe's school. I think about Meyer lying comatose in a bed in the Bonsucesso Hospital. I wonder how long they'll take to test his blood, and whether the doctors might find something that the drug-testers couldn't. And I wonder what kind of recovery Lucas Meyer might make – if he makes any kind of recovery at all.

CHAPTER 10

I WAKE UP AT 3 a.m. the following morning, to find the ceiling of our bedroom spinning and Juliana looking with concern into my opening eyes.

'It's just a dream, Rafael.'

The familiarity of her voice wraps around me and pulls me back from the night terrors. I realise that she has gently taken hold of my hand. I'm sweating and my heart is thumping.

When my pulse begins to slow, she says simply, 'You were calling out, Rafa.'

I don't remember the dream, but I know in my bones it was about Gilmore. Juliana fixes me a glass of orange juice and one for herself, and we sit in bed sipping the drink and listening to the stillness of the night. It's a familiar routine. It happens during the tough cases. The ones that chew me up. Here I am, days from retirement, and I have never cared more.

'Don't tell Paz.'

Juliana's delicate fingers wrap around my forearm.

'Tell her what? That you care?'

I shrug.

'Just don't tell her. It won't help.'

We turn out the light and the conversation slows until we drift back into sleep. The second half of the night goes better, and by the time I meet Paz the next morning, the nightmare is a distant memory.

Like a ship weathering the storm, Casas Pedro has ridden the waves and bobbed back to equilibrium. The Olympic revellers from the opening night are gone and a sense of normality has returned. Paz is looking through the menu, even though she's eaten here a million times. Thiago, son of the famous Pedro, makes his way to our table and shakes my hand.

'Feijoada?' he asks, a pencil poised above his waiter's pad.

I give it a couple of seconds, to pretend that I'm not such a creature of habit.

'Why not?'

'With the fried cheese rolls?'

'Is there any other way?'

Paz rolls her eyes.

'How have you lived so long, Carvalho?'

Thiago smiles, and so do I.

Paz orders orange juice and toast. When Thiago is gone, she lights up a cigarette from her crushed pack of Belmonts.

'Sleep well?'

I look at her through the haze of smoke.

'Not really.'

'Me neither.'

She takes a lungful of nicotine and leans back in her plastic chair, looking around at the other diners.

'I can't understand how Gilmore and Meyer would have known each other? They're not teammates; they play different sports for different countries.'

'Different continents,' I agree.

Paz blows out smoke and frowns. Then she slips her fingers under the sleeve of her black vest and pulls at her bra strap, the way she always does when she's thinking.

'Maybe Jaffari's right about the performance-enhancing drugs. Maybe Gilmore was taking the same drug and they were both suffering side-effects and confiding in each other. You know, trying to work out how to deal with them?'

I shake my head.

'How would either of them know that the other one was taking the drug? They wouldn't advertise it. Jaffari said the main side-effect is paranoia. Therefore they're not going to talk over the phone about it. No way.'

Paz takes another drag on her cigarette, narrows her eyes and raises an eyebrow.

'Do you think Jaffari's right?'

'It's all speculation,' I tell her. 'A lot of assumptions. Who knows if he's right? Maybe they were plotting to kill the President.'

'With a javelin?'

'Just keeping our options open, Paz.'

Paz stubs out her cigarette as she spots Thiago approaching with the food. He arrives fully loaded and places toast and juice in front of Paz. The rest is for me.

'Jesus, Rafael.'

I smile. We eat. The feijoada stew tastes good: chunks of pork and beef falling apart as soon as my fork touches them.

'Maybe it's a coincidence,' Paz says suddenly.

'Maybe what is?'

She points to the table next to us. A man and a woman are sharing breakfast. Early twenties, I'd guess. They're well dressed. The woman is watching people passing by, the man is thumbing his phone, the way all young people seem to do these days. Then I see what Paz means. The woman is eating toast and drinking juice. The man has a plate of feijoada. Just like us.

'What are the odds?' Paz asks me. 'And what are the odds of Gilmore's attack and Meyer's attempted suicide, and the phone call between them, all being a coincidence, too? Can we rule that out altogether?'

I think about it for a minute. I think how much easier my life would be, if I could explain the problem away as one of life's weird and wonderful quirks. But I can't.

'Yeah,' I say. 'We're ruling out coincidence.'

Suddenly the table rattles as Paz's phone vibrates with an incoming call.

'Hello?'

She listens for twenty seconds, and is already pushing her chair back by the time she hangs up.

'Someone's shooting at the crowd in the arena,' she says. 'We've got to go now.'

PART 3

WITT AND ZOU

CHAPTER 11

THE NATIONAL SHOOTING CENTRE is twenty minutes from Casas Pedro. Fifteen, the way Paz is driving.

'Oliver Witt,' Paz says and pushes the pedal closer to the floor. 'Heard of him?'

I tell her I haven't.

'He's a target-shooter. A good one. Only he's not aiming at the targets right now, so they're evacuating the stadium.'

'Have there been any casualties?'

'He's been shooting into the air, punching holes in the roof. He hasn't hit anyone yet. Nobody's quite sure what he's doing.'

When we arrive, people are spilling out of every exit and escaping down the long, narrow road that runs behind the shooting galleries. The building stretches far into the distance and is organised in the simplest way imaginable. The exits are on our side of the building. The ranges are on the other. People come in one side, and competitors fire out of the other, except for Witt, who is firing wherever he damn well likes. Every few seconds another shot rings out, and people in the emerging crowd duck and scream.

Outside the main entrance, a Policia Militar SWAT team is kitting up with enough weapons to start a small war. Whatever Oliver Witt is trying to achieve, he's on a suicide mission, just as Gilmore had been. I push through the crowd.

'Let's get in there,' I tell Paz. Maybe I can get to Witt before the SWAT team. Inside, the place smells of fresh paint and burned cartridges. The corridor is tight, with breeze-block walls closing in on both sides. We're swimming against a tide of people still trying to escape. I recognise a face in the crowd jostling past me. It's the blonde woman who was talking to the Russian team at the wrestling venue. I turn on my heel to get a better look as she passes and collide with Paz, who is running fast to catch up with me.

'Did you see that?'

Paz thrusts a Kevlar vest at me.

'See what?'

I decide the conversation about the Russian girl can wait.

'What's the point of this?' I ask, fastening the protective vest around me. 'Witt is an Olympic shooter. If he aims at us, a vest won't help.'

'Try not to annoy him, then.'

Paz tries to raise a smile, but falters as the sound of gunfire cracks through the air. We scan the arena. The rows of blue seats in front of us are deserted. Coats, bags and food cartons are lying abandoned in the stands.

'Why didn't the other competitors shoot him?' Paz asks. 'They were all armed.'

Down below, athletes have grabbed what equipment they could and have run. Piles of kit bags and tripods tell the story of a sharp retreat.

'Because they were terrified, probably. They're not cops, Vitoria. They're not soldiers. They shoot at paper targets, and the targets don't usually shoot back.'

The air cracks again and we drop to the floor.

'Where is he?'

I can't see, so I don't answer. Instead, I stand up and call his name.

'Oliver?'

My voice echoes around the place. Time is pressing. The SWAT team won't be much longer. Witt emerges from the shadow of a huge scoreboard. He is at the far end of the gallery, little more than a black dot walking along the green no-man's-land between the shooting positions and the targets. He's holding a long-barrelled pistol at his side and raises his arm towards me as he approaches. My blood runs cold, but I hold it together. There's no point running now.

'Oliver Witt?'

He keeps walking, and as he comes closer, I can hear him muttering to himself. I remember what Jaffari said about drugs bringing on psychosis, and I wonder if it could explain Witt's behaviour. He fires off a couple of rounds, smashing two giant TV monitors at the far end of the gallery. Then he aims the gun at me again. I remember reading about Olympic pistols. They have tiny magazines. Five bullets. Maybe six. I can't remember. I start counting anyway. Two down. Three to go. Or maybe four.

He's moved close enough that I can make him out properly. He is not a handsome man. He's carrying a little too much weight and his face looks podgy. His eyes look a little small and his lips are thin, compared to the roundness of his face. He hasn't shaved and he looks as though he hasn't slept.

'I'm a policeman,' I tell him. 'We need to talk, because my colleagues are on the way. They're armed and they're itching to shoot you – you understand?'

In front of us, he sinks to his knees, the way a footballer does when he scores a great goal. Except that he's sobbing, and he turns the shaking barrel of the pistol towards his own temple.

'Maybe I can save them the trouble.'

A look in his eyes tells me he's not bluffing. It's a look of despair. Hopelessness. I sense Paz tensing up beside me, fearing the worst.

'I was the policeman who shot Tim Gilmore,' I say. I'm not sure why I tell him this, except that it feels like the right thing to do. Maybe it will change something up. Because what could be worse? 'I don't want to see another athlete die.'

A momentary wash of interest floods into Witt's previously lifeless eyes. It's enough to make him pause, which is enough to encourage me to keep talking.

'I had to make a choice,' I say, freewheeling. 'There was no other way to stop him, and I couldn't let him carry on. He was out of control. Kind of feels like you're out of control right now.'

The more I talk, the more Witt listens. I step out from behind the row of chairs and move slowly down the concrete stairway towards where he is kneeling. I reach the bottom of the flight and sit down on a plastic seat in the front row. I don't want to walk any closer because I don't want him to feel threatened. More to the point, I don't want him to put a bullet in me.

'I can help you,' I say earnestly. Something about the way he's holding himself changes. Whatever he had been planning to do, he's un-planning it in front of my eyes. 'Tell me what I can do to help?'

He looks at me, eye-to-eye. Man-to-man.

'And put the gun down, for Christ's sake,' I tell him. 'You're going to hurt somebody if you're not careful.'

I silently pray that he'll hear the warmth in my tone. Slowly Witt pulls the long pistol away from his temple. His trembling hand arcs gradually away from his head, and for a moment I am looking straight down the barrel into the gun's black heart. Witt leans slightly to one side and places the gun gently on the floor. I take a lungful of air and realise that I've been holding my breath for a long time. The oxygen hits my bloodstream and I feel my muscles unclench.

'What is it?' I ask him softly. 'What's going on?'

He shakes his head slowly, as if he can make no more sense of it than I can. Then he rolls his shoulders and takes a breath, and slowly brings his gaze up from the floor until he is staring straight at me. I can see a confession in his watery, red-rimmed eyes. Witt knows something, and I'm about to know it, too. But as he draws breath to speak, I watch in horror as at least six of his front teeth disappear, smashed out by a bullet from somewhere over my shoulder. The whip-crack of a firing pistol registers milliseconds afterwards, sharp and violent. It is a perfect shot, entering through his open mouth and severing his spine, forcing bone and sinew and skin and blood to fuse and flail, then push out of the back of his neck.

For a moment Witt's body holds, balanced in the praying position, and I can see his final confused and horrified emotions playing across his undamaged face. Then gravity finds a weak spot and pulls him face-down onto the cold green floor. A second shot cracks violently through the air behind me and I hear a second body hit the floor. The dead-weight slap of skin on unforgiving concrete chills my blood. I pull myself from my seat and spin, my heart cold with fear and my head full of Vitoria Paz.

CHAPTER 12

DETECTIVE VITORIA PAZ HAS been my partner for three years. Most mornings she's outside my house before eight. There isn't a month goes by that Juliana doesn't invite her over for Sunday lunch. Felipe, her boy, calls me Uncle Rafa. So when I hear the second shot crack through the air in the arena, I turn fast, dreading what I'm going to see.

What I see is the back of Paz's head. Intact. She's still on her feet. Just behind her, in the doorway that leads back to the deserted corridor, is the slumped shell of a woman. She is Asian. Chinese, maybe. Paz is already climbing towards her and I debate for a moment whether to follow her or whether to head down towards Oliver Witt. I'm not sure who's the hero and who's the villain. Besides, I don't imagine there will be much I can do for either of them.

A combination of duty and curiosity forces me up the steep steps behind Paz. I watched Witt die. I saw the back of his skull. I watched the life extinguish from his eyes as he fell. The woman who shot him had been behind me and I have no idea whether she's alive or dead.

Paz slows up before she's reached the shooter, which is a sure sign that she's beyond help. I understand why when I reach Paz's shoulder. The Asian woman is crumpled into the doorway. Her legs are splayed out at an unnatural angle, her knees twisted. Only the door jamb has kept her from falling completely. There is a high-powered competition rifle at her feet and a long-barrelled pistol still hanging from her right hand, her finger caught in the trigger.

'Competitor,' Paz says, straightening an identity lanyard around the woman's neck.

'That figures,' I say, looking back over my shoulder at Witt lying dead on the floor from one perfect shot. A pool of blood is gradually blooming around him.

'Chinese,' Paz reads. 'Zou Jaihui. Twenty-four years old.'

Paz takes her time examining the athlete's head. Her face is intact, but from behind it's a different story. She's missing a chunk from the back of her neck and the base of her skull. 'She shot him with the rifle and killed herself with the pistol,' Paz says. 'That much is obvious.'

I nod.

'So what do you think?'

Paz pauses.

'Maybe she was competing somewhere else in the arena, heard the commotion and decided to be a hero?'

'I don't think so. That wouldn't explain why she then killed herself.'

Behind the stricken body of the Chinese athlete, the sound of heavy boots begins to reverberate along the deserted corridor. The SWAT team is arriving.

'Come on, then,' Paz says. 'What's your theory?'

I look down at the girl, and the madness of it all makes me angry. Two more athletes wasted in the prime of their lives.

'She's either a rifle star or a pistol star. She's not both. My guess is rifle, judging by the job she did on Witt. So why is she carrying both guns?'

Paz looks blankly at me.

'You tell me.'

'Because she came here to do a job. She's come equipped. A rifle for him and a pistol for herself.'

'A paid assassin?'

'No, but I think she knew him. I think she knew Witt was going to kill himself. He put the gun to his head, after all. And when he couldn't finish the job, she did it for him.'

'And for herself,' Paz says.

I nod. The SWAT team bursts through an entrance adjacent to ours and fans out into the arena. I've already pulled my badge out from my pocket, and I hold it above my head. Paz does the same.

'Too late,' I call to the team of black-clad officers. 'The woman up here shot the guy down there. We saw it happen. You fill in the form and I'll sign it.'

The corners of Paz's mouth lift for a split second, and then she returns to her steely evaluation of the scene.

'What makes you think she knew Witt?'

I crouch down so that my eyes are at the same level as Zou Jaihui. Paz hears both of my knees crack on the way down, but she's kind enough to ignore it.

'This girl was careful how she killed herself,' I tell Paz. 'She shot herself through the mouth. She didn't touch her features. She looks like she's asleep.'

Paz looks at the slack features of the slumped shooter.

'Meaning what?' Paz asks urgently as the SWAT team approaches.

'Meaning she didn't want to put her relatives through the pain of identifying a disfigured face.'

'Same as most suicides, probably.'

I smile for a moment.

'Sure,' I tell her. 'But Zou did the same for Witt. Perfect aim. Perfect shot. Straight through the back of his throat, without a speck of blood on his face. She didn't want to damage him any more than she wanted to damage herself. Makes me think she cared about him.'

'*She cared about him?* Carvalho, the back of his skull is missing.'

'Yeah, but she never saw that, did she? The simplest job would have been three rifle shots, dead centre. She'd have taken out everything from the neck up. But she didn't do that. She went to the trouble of aiming through his mouth with a single shot. Maybe she didn't want to see him broken. My guess is: whatever was driving Oliver Witt crazy, I'll bet you that Zou Jaihui knew all about it.'

CHAPTER 13

THREE PARAMEDICS RUSH TOWARDS us as we head wearily out of the arena. They're moving fast, pumped with adrenalin.

'No rush,' I tell them.

As we walk back through the exit, I flash back to the blonde woman who had been pushing past us as we arrived.

'Yeah, I saw her,' Paz says. 'A coincidence?'

I scowl.

'We ruled out coincidence, remember?'

Before Paz can apologise, her phone rings.

'Meyer's bloods,' she says when the call ends. 'Nothing unusual, apart from the sleeping pills.'

'Well, if he was hooked on an undetectable drug, I guess it wouldn't show up. His body could be pumped full of something and we wouldn't know.'

We drive back across town without saying much, both of us turning over the shootings in our minds. I watch the mid-morning sun warming the waters of Guanabara Bay, the huge expanse of sea lapping against Rio's golden shore. The sun warms the water, and the sand, and the concrete, and the lush vegetation, and finally the soaring rock of Sugarloaf, and Christ the Redeemer as he reaches out to gather in the day.

I think about the split second when I shot Tim Gilmore. The confusion of the scene. I think about Meyer's lonely apartment and his mottled blue skin. I think of Witt, angry and afraid like a wounded animal. And of Zou, and the terrible sound her body made when it slumped to the floor.

'No more,' I say to myself as much as to Paz. And I mean it.

Twenty minutes later, I'm still pulling at threads and trying to make connections between the four athletes, as Paz drives the Fiat through the grey corrugated fortress gates to the police compound. The car park is surrounded by a ten-foot-high white brick wall, and the building itself is low-slung, with windows made of iron slats.

'Our little Tent of Miracles,' I say to Paz and she looks at me blankly. 'Come on,' I tell her. 'Jorge Amado. Born 1912. Brazil's greatest writer?'

No reaction. I roll my eyes. This is our thing. I tell her about the great writers and our country's history. She tells me about soap operas and reality TV.

'Oh yeah,' she says suddenly. '*Jorge Amado. 1912.* Didn't you go to school with him, Carvalho?'

I swipe my badge across the security door and hear the heavy lock clunk open as Paz grins and pushes past me into the building. Inside there is a long, dreary corridor that aims for the heart of the station. It's all walls and ceilings. No doors. No windows. No natural light. Nothing but stale air.

'Find out what you can about Witt,' I say as we walk. 'If there's anything in this drugs theory, then he was showing all the right signs. See if you can find a connection with Gilmore.'

'Sure. Am I investigating him as a perpetrator or a victim?'

Our feet thud on the worn carpet and the muffled sound bounces off the stark grey walls.

'Not sure.'

'And Zou Jaihui?'

That's an even tougher call.

'Perp for now. But let's see what comes out in the wash. I can't help thinking they're all in something together.'

We emerge into the main processing area. I call it 'the bear pit'. In the centre are a handful of desks covered by a mountain of files. The files are surrounded by coffee cups and evidence bags, and every phone is ringing off the hook. Cases are being discussed, people are shouting. Criminals are being processed. We pause in the doorway, preparing, as if we're about to jump from the back of a plane.

'Find a connection, Paz.'

'Okay.'

'And the blonde girl. Try to find out who she is.'

Paz turns to look at me.

'You think she knows something?'

I take a long breath and think about it, trying to block out the bedlam.

'Maybe.'

Paz smiles her light-bulb smile.

'What are you going to do, exactly?'

I look across the room through the crowd and lock eyes with the Captain, who looks like he's spoiling for a fight.

'Me? I'm going to buy us some time.'

CHAPTER 14

IT IS NOT AN easy thing to accept the authority of a younger man. However, the older I've become, the more I've had to get used to it. Silva is not a bad captain. But he is young. And right now he's nervous.

'You know this department is being watched?' he says.

He's trying to stay level, and I guess I appreciate the effort.

'Let me ask you a question,' I say. 'Would you rather I'd let Gilmore smash his javelin through the President?'

'That doesn't change the fact, Carvalho. You shot an athlete.'

'Gilmore killed himself, when he took aim at the President. What I'm doing is trying to work out why.'

'And in the meantime two more athletes are dead, and another one is barely alive.'

'They're connected.'

'I don't doubt it, Carvalho,' Silva tells me. 'But what's the deal? Why's it happening? How many more are going to die?'

'None.'

Captain Silva scowls.

'How do you know?'

I stare through the glass. Paz has taken a seat at one of the desks in the pit, and I watch her as Silva closes his office door.

'I need something solid,' Silva says. 'I trust you, Carvalho, but there is a wave of shit heading your way. My boss. *His* boss. They're gunning for someone, and right now you're in the cross-hairs.'

'Nothing new.'

'Help me to help you. What do you have?'

I pull up a chair and fall gracelessly into it. I'm tired and I'm beyond trying to hide my years from my younger boss.

'I don't know, Marcelo. It might be drugs.'

'It might be drugs?'

'Maybe. Lucas Meyer's psychologist is in town. He says Meyer was taking something that was making him paranoid.'

'Was there anything in the tox report?'

I shake my head.

'But there wouldn't be, according to the psychologist. He says it's untraceable.'

'You buy that?'

'Well, they all showed signs of paranoia.'

'And the Chinese girl?'

I raise my palms.

'Who knows? Paz is digging up some background.'

Silva looks hard at me.

'She needs to dig fast, understand?'

'She's digging right now.'

Silva stays quiet for a moment.

'What if it's something else?'

'Like what?'

'Well, terrorism, for example. The Mayor's office is on the phone every hour asking about security.'

'If Gilmore was a terrorist, he wasn't a very good one. He was never going to succeed. If I hadn't shot him, somebody else would have. Witt didn't seem as if he actually wanted to shoot anyone. Zou shot Witt, and Meyer tried to kill himself. Do they sound like terrorists to you?'

'Okay,' Silva concedes. 'So it's drugs?'

'I don't know for sure, Marcelo. I'm working on it.'

The Captain sighs.

'Well, as I say . . . work fast.'

Paz is behind a stack of files and an ancient computer screen when I get back to the bear pit. She puts the phone down as I approach. She looks stressed.

'Bad news?'

'What?'

'The phone call. Was it bad news?'

'Oh – no, it was Hunter Brown. Gilmore's trainer. I told him what Jaffari said about performance-enhancing drugs, but Brown's convinced Gilmore wasn't taking anything.'

'Well, as a coach he's hardly going to want to admit something like that.'

'True, but I pushed him hard. I put him out of the frame, asked him if Gilmore could have been taking something without him knowing. But he's pretty sure Gilmore was clean.'

I call Meyer's coach while Paz talks to Oliver Witt's team. We both get the same answer. No drugs. No clues. They're sure their athletes were clean.

'Do you believe them?' Paz asks, once we've compared notes.

I shrug.

'Do you?'

I call the Chinese camp, hoping to talk to Zou's coach. The phone rings for ever, and when someone eventually answers, they're no help at all. The woman at the Chinese camp claims she doesn't know Zou's coach. Claims she doesn't know Zou. Her answers are slippery and evasive. She says she doesn't understand many of my questions, and when she does understand, she doesn't have any authority to answer. I don't like her, and she makes it obvious that she doesn't like me.

'First job tomorrow,' I tell Paz as I put the phone down, 'let's go and turn the Chinese camp upside down.'

CHAPTER 15

TWELVE HOURS LATER, PAZ is sucking on another early-morning cigarette as her Fiat speeds towards the Olympic Village. From the corner of her mouth she says, 'Do you know how much money China has invested in Brazil since we got the Olympic Games?'

I can tell she is pleased with herself. This is the kind of information I usually push on her while we're driving, but today she has the upper hand.

'Fifty-three billion US dollars,' she says. 'Can you believe that?'

I think about the miles of new tarmac and the soaring new buildings all over town.

'I guess I can.'

I'm distracted by three boys playing in the dust at the side of the road ahead. Just like I used to play when I was a kid.

'There's another two hundred and fifty billion dollars on the way. I saw it on the news. You know that's why Zou is going to matter, right?'

A football rolls into the road in front of us and one of the boys bolts after it. My foot slams at an imaginary brake pedal as Paz swerves, but the boy stays on the kerb and we sail on past.

'They all matter, Paz.'

She turns her head and looks at me longer than she should while she's driving, before eventually turning back to the road. She blows out smoke and says, 'I know, Carvalho.'

When we arrive, the Chinese camp is a hive of activity. Six gleaming coaches are snaked along the kerb outside the high-rise athletes' block, and the entire Chinese team appears to be surrounding them. We spend five minutes asking after Zou's coach. Eventually Paz finds her on the other side of the crowd. I force my way through and Paz introduces me.

'This is Chao Ling.'

The woman next to Paz is compact and hard; paper-thin skin stretches over her taut muscles and thin blue veins. She looks through me and around me all at once, her clear eyes suggesting a smart brain.

'What's happening?'

She tilts her angular face to meet my question, and lingers on my features for a moment before she draws breath to answer.

'We're all moving out.'

'I can see that.'

I remember what Paz said in the car: *That's why Zou is going to matter.*

Chao says, 'We're moving out because you cannot protect us.'

Her lips seal tightly together and she seems hostile. She studies me, waiting to see how I'll respond to her accusation. The crowd continues to mill around us. Full retreat. Confused athletes ship holdalls and equipment into the yawning underbellies of the coaches.

I don't know whether I trust Chao. Maybe it's true that her federation is protecting its athletes from harm. But from years of chasing criminals, I've learned that people who run away are usually guilty of something. Maybe Zou was doping. Maybe she wasn't alone in the Chinese camp. That would be a reason for the team to run.

'The Games are cursed,' Chao says drily.

I glance at Paz. *That's a theory we haven't considered.* I hold Chao Ling's gaze a little longer, but she gives nothing away.

'We need to see Zou Jaihui's room.'

Zou Jaihui's apartment is eight floors up and is just like Gilmore's place, and Meyer's. The scene is becoming depressingly familiar. Paz moves around, noting anything that might be of interest, and ends up in the bathroom where she finds a clutch of medications, which she starts bagging up for testing. Chao Ling stares from the doorway as if we're grave-robbers. The news is flickering from a tiny television on the wall in the open-plan kitchen. The screen is showing grainy mobile-phone coverage of Oliver Witt opening fire in the shooting arena. Paz emerges from the bathroom and watches the report over my shoulder.

'You think she saw the first reports and headed down to the arena?'

I shake my head.

'She was there too soon. She must have been nearby.'

Unwashed crockery waits by the sink and there's a half-finished game of mah-jong on the kitchen table. Life, interrupted. Zou has turned the windowsill into a temporary bookshelf and, beyond the books, there's a breathtaking view of the Olympic Village and the city beyond. I run a finger across the spines of the books. I'm three-quarters along when I stop. One of them is out of place. It's written in Portuguese and the rest are Chinese. Curious, I pull it out. It's Paolo Coelho.

'*O Alquimista*,' Paz says.

I leaf through it and a bookmark falls from its page. I pick it up and on it is a telephone number. My heart skips. It's the same number that we found in Tim Gilmore's apartment. On this paper, in black and white, is concrete proof that all of this is connected.

CHAPTER 16

'IT'S PROBABLY THEIR DEALER'S number,' Paz says as we walk back to the car. 'Chao Ling was pretty quiet when you told her it matched the one in Gilmore's apartment.'

'That doesn't mean she knows anything. She's probably scared to death.'

I watch Paz trying to summon up sympathy for Chao, without much success, as we fight our way through the bottleneck of departing athletes. The mid-morning sun is hot on the side of my face and the feeling of bodies crushing in on us is unwelcome. I check my Casio: 11.30 a.m.

'Fancy a Coke?'

Paz nods, and we muscle through the rest of the crowd and duck into a brand-new cafeteria on the corner of the block. The walls are painted in the same calm magnolia as the athletes' apartments, and the owner has compensated by scattering garish beanbags across the polished-concrete floor. The counter is dominated by a chrome coffee machine. I order the soda and head back to Paz. She's settled in the corner of the room and has the good grace not to laugh as I slump into a lurid green beanbag that matches hers.

'Some people will think this is Brazil,' Paz says sadly. Her eyes scan the walls, which feature overblown prints of iconic Rio scenes. One is a sunrise over Sugarloaf, and another features bathers on the Copacabana sands. Between the prints, TV screens are showing the latest action from the Games.

'What do you think about Zou now?'

I shrug.

'Well, she's the connection that we didn't have before. Gilmore led to Meyer, Meyer led to Witt, and Witt gave us Zou. The phone number connects the start and the end. It tells us that none of this is a coincidence.'

Paz pulls out her mobile phone and hits redial. She's been calling the number every couple of hours since we found it in Gilmore's apartment. It rings out, as it has every time.

'Well, that tells us nothing.'

I'm not so sure.

'It tells us that whoever's at the end of the phone is very cautious.'

'Or dead,' Paz says, throwing up her hands hopelessly. I smile, because we both know Paz doesn't give up as easily as that.

'They can't be dead, because the phone isn't dead. It's ringing out. Someone's charging it. They're charging it because they're expecting someone to call.'

Paz is halfway down her Coke, chewing on her straw as she thinks.

'Got to be a dealer,' she says. 'But how are we going to find them?'

I look at her, sprawled out on the bright-green beanbag like a kid. She's drinking soda and twisting to get comfortable. If I were twenty years younger, I'd enjoy sticking around and watching Paz grow. She's tenacious and restless, and she's going to be a very good cop.

'I don't know how we're going to find them, Paz.'

The TV screen on the wall catches my eye. It's showing the early session of the boxing at the Riocentro Pavilion. Two women are toe-to-toe when the bell rings, and they turn and head back to their corners. The TV station replays the biggest shots of the round, and super-slo-mo pictures show sweat exploding from the women's contorted faces. Then the camera pans out and takes in the crowd, hundreds of faces in the dark. In the front row, conspicuous between the muscle-bound boxing coaches, is the tiny blonde girl in a white tracksuit. Paz spots her, too.

'Who *is* that woman?'

I hold up Zou's bookmark.

'I don't know. But I wonder if this is her number?'

CHAPTER 17

THE RIOCENTRO IS HUMMING when we arrive almost thirty minutes later, the roar of the crowd crashing over us like an ebbing tide. There are new fighters in the ring, but the woman in the white tracksuit is still in the front row, watching the action on the canvas square in the centre of the arena.

Paz pulls out her phone and dials the number we found in Zou's apartment. I watch the blonde-haired woman, waiting for the moment when she reaches into her pocket and pulls out her phone. The moment she hangs herself. But it doesn't happen. She sits watching the fight without moving, and Paz looks forlorn as her phone rings out.

'Let's talk to her anyway.'

We make our way down the stairs towards the ring. The noise is building to a crescendo as the fight reaches its most critical phase. Indian and Irish flags hang above the ring as the two fighters circle below in perpetual motion, their bodies slick with endeavour. We reach the front just as the timekeeper's bell rings shrilly above the noise of the crowd. The crowd howls as the women's scores light up on the giant central display, and the fighters move back to their corners to be patched up.

We make our way along the front row until we reach the woman in white.

'Detectives Carvalho and Paz,' I say. 'Can we have a word, please?'

The woman looks at me blankly, and as I lean in so that she can hear me better above the crowd, the guy next to her decides to intervene. He's bigger than me. A lot bigger. So I don't let him up. I poke two stern fingers where his chest meets his throat and push him straight back down into his seat. With my other hand, I show him my badge. The combination of physical and psychological pressure does the job. Which is good because he's a colossus. I lead the blonde out of the arena, and Paz brings up the rear. We head through doors and out into a brightly lit service corridor. I slow up and turn to face her, Paz arriving at my elbow.

'What's your name?'

She looks from me to Paz and back again.

'Galina Orlov.'

She pulls her official credentials from around her neck and hands them to me for examination. The name on her ID card matches, as does the picture of her looking dispassionately into the camera. When I look up, she's gazing at me with the exact same stare. Paz studies her credentials for a moment and then looks up at the woman in front of us.

'Russian?'

The girl nods. In the bright light, she looks young and vital. Her grey eyes are alive and alert, her skin is almost pearlescent and her prominent cheekbones are helped by subtle rouge.

'You're a diver?'

'Yes. Can I ask what this is about?'

Paz hands her official pass back, and the girl pulls the lanyard over her head without breaking eye contact.

'Why are you at the boxing, if you're a diver? Shouldn't you be at the pool?'

'I'm injured,' she says, turning back to face me. 'I'll be at the pool later.'

'We saw you in the shooting centre yesterday. And at the wrestling. We've been investigating athletes in those sports.'

'There are nine thousand people back there,' Orlov says, pointing over my shoulder and back into the Riocentro Pavilion. 'I'm sure some of them were at the wrestling, too. Is that a crime now?'

Her voice is earnest.

'It's no crime. But I'm investigating the deaths of Zou Jaihui and Oliver Witt, and the injury to Lucas Meyer. You've seen all three of them in the past few days. I'm wondering if that's just a coincidence?'

'It's very sad.'

I agree with her.

'But, as I told you, I'm injured,' she continues. 'I trained for four years to be here, and last month I tore a muscle in my leg. So now I can't dive. Understand?'

Suddenly her passive features are alive, her eyes welling and her pale brow furrowing. She takes a breath, straightens her back and blinks away the threat of tears.

'The Russian team asked me to travel to Brazil anyway. Asked me to look after our team's welfare. So now I make sure someone fixes their dripping taps, and I make sure they have spare shoelaces. Glamorous stuff. It's not really much of a job, but they wanted to soften the blow.'

Her pale lips break into a brave smile, and for a moment I can feel her pain.

'So you've been everywhere because . . . ?'

'Because I'm checking up on my teammates. Are they happy? Are they stressed? I flutter between them to find out. I'm a butterfly.'

She flutters her eyelashes and even Paz smiles. It strikes me that she's young, and she's worked hard, and she's had a hell of a dream taken away from her.

'We think Tim Gilmore, Lucas Meyer, Oliver Witt and Zou Jaihui might have been experiencing side-effects from a performance-enhancing drug. Did you hear anything about that?'

Orlov doesn't look too keen to help.

'Three of them are dead,' I push. 'One of them is never going to be the same again. If you know something, you should say.'

'I don't know anything.'

'You didn't hear anything?'

She shakes her head.

'I didn't hear anything.'

'See anything?'

'Nope.'

Suddenly she's standing square-on to me, her arms folded and her guard up.

Paz steps between us.

'Can I check your bag?'

Orlov's brow lowers again.

'Do I have a choice?'

'Have you got something to hide?'

The blonde athlete misses a beat, as if what she really wants to say is *Fuck you*, but after a moment she looks from Paz to me and shrugs.

'I don't have anything to hide,' she says. 'But, also, this isn't a police state. So no, you cannot check my bag.'

She cocks her head slightly to one side, waiting to see what will happen next. Like it's a game. I sigh, long and hard.

'Let me explain to you what's going to happen next—'

She rolls her eyes and cuts me off.

'I know what's going to happen. You'll get a warrant, you'll seize my bag and you'll break down my door in the night. I know this stuff. It doesn't scare me, Detective Carvalho.'

'No,' I say wearily. 'That's not what's going to happen. What's going to happen is that you'll make our lives difficult, because you think that's what we're doing to you. I'm guessing your parents lived through the worst years of the KGB, so you probably don't like cops much. You'll go home tonight and smile, because you'll think you gave two officious cops the runaround and stood up to authority, right?'

Her eyes narrow.

'But athletes are dying, Galina. Maybe because of a new drug. A drug that might be hidden away in your bag while you're butterflying between venues, for all I know.'

She looks down at her bag and back up at me.

'The truth is that you can open your bag and prove you're innocent right now, or you can yank my chain and I can go away and investigate you. The choice is yours. However, while you're giving me the runaround, another athlete could be dying. And I will not kick your door down in the middle of the night, but I swear to God that I will knock courteously in the morning with an envelope full of pictures of the next person who dies while you're jerking us around.'

She says nothing.

'That's a promise.'

I wait in silence for her to make a decision. Eventually she blows out a long breath and opens her bag. She pulls out her lipgloss and applies it, while holding the bag for Paz to examine. I understand that it's humiliating and, when it's done, I apologise.

'I hope you will forgive us,' I tell her. 'And when you're back in Russia thinking about us, remember that we were doing what we could to keep your teammates safe.'

Galina Orlov replaces the top of her lipgloss in silence and closes the bag, her pretty face suddenly Slavic and inscrutable.

'Can I go?'

I tell her she can. Once she is gone, Paz thrusts her hands into her pockets and blows out in exasperation.

'There goes our only lead,' she says. 'Now what?'

CHAPTER 18

NEXT MORNING, JULIANA WAKES me long after dawn with hot coffee and a message from work.

'Paz called. She's running late. She's dropping Felipe at school this morning. I thought I'd leave you to sleep. I can drive you to meet her.'

When I arrive at the school, I wonder if Paz has been dreaming too, because she looks tired and careworn.

'Let's go eat,' she says. 'Food fixes everything.'

There's a street vendor selling hot food halfway between Felipe's school and the police station. Paz pulls over and I order two egg-and-meat burgers and we eat them at the side of the road.

'This investigation is killing my diet.'

I look up from my burger.

'Tastes good, though, right?'

We get stuck in, the egg yolk bursting as I bite into my burger. It's impossible for my mood not to lift.

'What's the plan?'

I take another bite of my burger to buy some time. I have a mobile-phone number that links Gilmore to Zou, and a chain of events that link both of them to Meyer and Witt. But I can't trace the mobile and nobody's picking up the phone. We had a suspect in Galina Orlov, but she's fallen through. So the truth is: I don't have a plan.

I wipe my mouth with the back of my hand and take a breath, but before I get a chance to say anything, my phone rings. It's the precinct. There's been a report that a British athlete is threatening to jump from the Vista Chinesa, a huge bamboo pagoda up in the mountains.

'New plan,' I tell Paz as we head back to the car. 'The guy's name is Steve Lewis, and apparently he knows why Oliver Witt went crazy.'

PART 4

STEVE LEWIS

CHAPTER 19

PAZ IS STILL EATING her burger as she drives hard along the Alto da Boa Vista. We're climbing away from the sea and into the mountains, the air getting cooler and thinner as we go.

'Well, that explains why he's at the Vista Chinesa,' I say from the passenger seat as I scroll through an Internet search. 'Steve Lewis is a British cyclist. The pagoda is on the route of the road race.'

'Jesus!' says Paz, glancing across at my screen. 'Look at those thighs. They're like tree trunks.'

Her phone rings on the dashboard. She has the steering wheel in one hand and her burger in the other, so I reach over and answer it for her. It's bad news.

'Meyer's dead,' I tell her when I hang up. 'He picked up an infection in the hospital. Off the record, the doctors are saying it might have been the best thing for him. His liver and kidneys were ruined, and probably his brain, too. If he'd ever come round, it's unlikely he could have told us anything.'

Another dead athlete. At the wheel, Paz is looking the same way I feel. Gutted.

'Autopsy?'

I nod.

'But they're not expecting anything illuminating. The bloods have already been done, and nothing has come back from the pathologist. If he was taking an undetectable drug, then it did what it said on the tin.'

Paz is driving hard and the tyres of the Fiat slide and complain as we round a tight bend. When we straighten up, we're driving straight into the sun. Paz squints and pulls down the visor. The Vista Chinesa comes into view moments later, a two-storey hexagonal structure clinging to the edge of the jutting mountain rock and looking out over all of Rio. A clutch of thin-wheeled bicycles are resting against the bollards, and a huddle of guys in Lycra are waiting inside the pagoda. They head towards us as we get out of the car. The first guy to reach us is the only one not wearing Lycra.

'Thank Christ you're here,' he says, and introduces himself as the team manager. 'I'm Adam Wilson. We're on a time trial, but something's gone wrong.'

'What, exactly?'

He struggles to put it into words.

'Not sure. It's Steve Lewis. He's on the wrong side of the barrier.'

'How long has he been there?'

The coach looks at his watch.

'Fifteen minutes. Maybe twenty.'

I leave Paz to deal with Wilson, and head to the barrier. I've already made a promise: no more athletes are going to die. *Steve Lewis is not going to die.* I climb straight over the barrier, without stopping to think. There's a short strip of rough-hewn earth beyond the bamboo, and after that, it's a sheer drop. Lewis is stock-still, perched right on the edge. He's contemplating the horizon, his knees drawn close to his chest, his thin arms pulling tight across his shins.

'Steve?'

I move slowly towards him, but he tenses and pushes out towards the edge as I approach.

'Stay the fuck where you are,' he says. 'Stay the *fuck* where you are!'

He turns and looks me in the eye and I know, without doubt, that he's not bluffing.

CHAPTER 20

I SIT DOWN ON the floor a few yards from Lewis. It feels like the right thing to do. His eyes flick between me and the terrifying drop. For a while I say nothing. I want the dust of my arrival to settle, before I start in on him.

'I love this view,' I say eventually.

There's no reaction, but I know he's listening.

'See the church right on the horizon?'

His head turns a fraction of a degree towards me, his eyes wide and scared.

'I married my wife there. Forty years ago. You think you're scared sitting up here? You should have seen me at the front of that church. I couldn't breathe, I was so scared. You know why? Because she was perfect. She still is. I couldn't believe she'd get all the way down the aisle without changing her mind.'

Lewis turns to look at me, his hair blowing in the wind. His cheeks are tear-stained, and his watery blue eyes flick between me and the church on the horizon.

'You still together?'

I smile.

'We are. I still don't know what she sees in me.'

Lewis smiles weakly. He takes a deep breath and shakes his head.

'Am I safe?'

It strikes me as an odd question from a guy who has climbed over a safety barrier towards a sheer drop, but I nod earnestly. Reassured, he turns back to the view. The wind drops and the heat picks up, and Lewis does nothing. I loosen my collar as the still air begins to stifle me. After a long minute, the sense of time passing becomes too much for me and I force the issue by edging closer. I realise immediately that it's a mistake. Too much, too soon. He shuffles further out, and some of the rock beneath him gives way. He scrabbles backwards, clawing frantically at the rock and the dirt, but gravity is against him and he slides hopelessly over the edge until his foot catches in a tree root. He kicks out with his powerful legs and is pushed back onto solid ground. I can see his chest pumping and the veins in his neck pulsing with adrenalin-fuelled blood. I've learned something: he doesn't want to die. That's something I can work with.

'Are you on drugs, Steve?'

'No.'

He looks confused by the question.

'You're the fifth athlete to act like this,' I tell him. 'The other four are dead.'

Two hawks circle on the thermals a few yards in front of us, scanning the ground far below them.

'I know about the others.'

'You know what, exactly?'

Lewis says nothing, his taut features struggling to settle on a single emotion. We are alone on the ledge, apart from the hawks, and the gods. Steve Lewis has a secret, and only I can unlock it.

'When I was a rookie cop,' I tell him, 'I used to feel a hell of a lot of pressure. Back then, Rio was even more dangerous than it is today, if you can believe that? I lost friends, and I beat myself up for not saving them. I felt a hell of a lot of pressure, you understand?'

Lewis raises his head just enough to acknowledge what I'm saying.

'You know what I did? I used to cry in the shower, where nobody could see me and nobody could judge me. I'm not ashamed to admit it.'

The cyclist turns his head towards me and our eyes lock.

'Pressure is a button,' he says.

'Sure,' I tell him. 'But you can switch it on or off. That's your choice.'

Lewis visibly relaxes, his back slumping slightly and his breathing slowing. I smile, because I get the feeling those few words just saved Steve Lewis's life. Behind me, Lewis's coach calls to him, and I realise for the first time that we have an audience.

'Time to come back over, Steve,' he says. 'We're all waiting for you, fella. You're scaring the shit out of us.'

On the edge of the cliff, Steve Lewis starts to cry. He drops his head and weeps as he watches the hawks riding the thermals. His Lycra-clad ribs shake as he sobs.

'Take it easy,' I tell him.

I move towards him and get an arm under him. It's the point of no return. If he decides to go over the edge now, then I'm going over, too. I clasp his hand in mine, and he leans into me. We both breathe a sigh of relief. I drag him back from the precipice, and he scrambles to his feet. I put an arm around his waist and guide him back to the bamboo barrier, where his coach gets an arm around his neck and grabs a hold of him as if he's never going to let go.

Once I'm on the other side of the barrier, it takes me five seconds to register that Paz has gone.

'She left in a hurry,' Wilson says, as I give Steve Lewis a bear hug and tell him everything's going to be fine. 'She told me to tell you she was heading for Vila Cruzeiro.'

I stop short. Vila Cruzeiro is not a good place to visit alone.

'Did she say why?'

'Something about her boy,' Wilson says apologetically. 'She seemed panicked. She wasn't very clear.'

I have to go. Right now. I turn back to Lewis and look him straight in the eye. I mention a name that has been rattling around my head for the last five minutes, and watch his face for a reaction. He looks at me blankly, and then slowly but surely he nods. And all of my suspicions are confirmed.

CHAPTER 21

I PULL OUT MY mobile as I walk away from the cyclists, scrolling to Paz's number and hitting green. A single bleep. *No damn signal.* There is a slow stream of traffic rolling past the Vista Chinesa, and I hold my badge aloft and head out into the road. The first car to stop is a Mercedes SUV.

The driver – a woman in her late twenties – looks relieved that I'm a cop and not a carjacker and, within seconds, I'm powering the SUV back down the asphalt towards the city. I try Paz's number again, but there's still no signal. I put my foot down hard and the SUV lurches forward. I cut corners. I slam into pavements. I'm heading for a street in the Vila Cruzeiro, a slum built on a rubbish dump outside Rio de Janeiro. As I drive, I find myself thinking about Paz's car, and the tiny holes in the foam in her passenger seat, and Felipe's tiny fingers. Every image gets me pushing harder on the accelerator.

Vila Cruzeiro is a grim place, full of red-brick huts holding each other up, and kids playing football in the dusty streets. Bathtubs on the roofs slowly collect rainwater for residents below. The place feels lawless, and I know I should wait for backup, but I can't. Paz is already charging headlong into trouble and I'm her partner. I'm not waiting for anyone.

I pass the garish Haas & Hahn block, painted in vivid carnival colours by crazy Dutch artists, then I plunge back into the red-brick and grey-slab concrete. I watch small children – the eyes and ears of the favela – receding into alleyways. If feels like the clock is already ticking.

I cruise for two minutes before I spot Paz's car, parked outside a dilapidated place with a barbed-wire roof and a crumbling façade. There is movement behind the grimy first-floor windows and I waste no time getting inside. I slam through the rotten wooden front door – peeling paint exploding as I kick. Pain shoots through my knee and I recall the long list of doors I've smashed through during my career. How easy it used to be. How worn I have become. I wonder if this will be the very last time.

'Police!'

Upstairs there is movement on bare floorboards. People moving into position. I pull my gun and take the creaking stairs two at a time. I emerge into the half light of the dirty upstairs room and find a man sitting in an easy chair. It's Rahim Jaffari, Lucas Meyer's psychologist. His cropped white hair and taut olive skin are unmistakable, even in the gloom.

Jaffari is smiling because he knows I can't shoot him. He is holding Felipe in front of him, drawing the small boy up by grabbing a fistful of his hair, using his tiny body as a human shield. His own gun is pressed against Felipe's delicate temple.

'You are the link between all of the athletes.'

He nods, and his lips curl into a satisfied smile. I want to hammer it right off his smug face, but he's holding a gun to Paz's boy's head. So I take a breath.

'We knew you were Meyer's psychologist when we took your call at the hospital. I bet you cursed your luck when you realised you were talking to a police officer. And I also know you worked with Steve Lewis, the cyclist.'

Jaffari looks intrigued.

'I found him on the side of a cliff. He told me that pressure is a button. You said the same thing, back at the Belmond hotel.'

Jaffari gives me a concessionary nod, before relaxing back into his chair, pulling Felipe with him. The boy looks drugged and docile.

'Well, I've got bad news for you. Lewis didn't jump. I talked him down. Whatever you've been doing, he will testify against you. I'll see to that.'

I catch a glimpse of Paz in the shadows. Her face looks bruised, but her eyes are burning with anger. She's not interested in people testifying against Rahim Jaffari. She wants him to die, today, in this room. I look back at how he's holding Felipe by the hair, and part of me hopes that Paz gets her way.

'If I was a betting man,' I tell Jaffari, 'I would lay money on the telephone number we found in Gilmore's apartment and Zou's place being yours.'

He smiles again, glances at a handset on the table next to him and presses a finger to his lips. I pull out my own mobile and dial. We both watch the phone on the table, but nothing happens.

'It's turned off, smart guy,' Jaffari says smugly. 'I don't want your friends tracing it.'

I shove my phone back into my pocket and look at the small boy Jaffari is holding in front of him. The boy who calls me Uncle Rafa. Behind Paz, I can see the red dot of a recording camera in the darkness.

'Tell me what you've done.'

Jaffari shrugs.

'It will go in your favour.'

He laughs.

'Nothing will go in my favour,' he says. 'But I'll tell you anyway. I need to tell you, because the world needs to know. That's why I've done it.'

'You killed four athletes,' I prompt.

'No. They killed themselves. I just told them that they should.'

I'm struggling to see the difference.

'Ever hear of Abu Ghraib prison?' he asks, and his tone is that of a man settling in for the long haul. 'I grew up in Iraq, and when the war came – when the Americans came – my brother was dragged off to Abu Ghraib. Back then, I had never heard of the place, either. Now everyone in Iraq knows the name. They tortured people there. They tortured my brother. They broke his bones. They electrocuted him three times. They raped him. And then they went back to their wives and their children, like heroes.'

Jaffari is still calm, but his voice has turned ice-cold.

'I wanted to know how any person could do that. Especially to my brother, who was a good man. So I studied psychology and psychiatry. First in Baghdad, and then in Lisbon. I began to practise. I wanted to learn about the evils people will do under pressure.'

'And it's all led to this?'

I push him, even though I'm not sure what *this* is.

'These are the world's strongest athletes,' Jaffari says. 'They are the pinnacle of human achievement. They run faster, throw further, jump higher. They are the perfect experiment. They are the very best of humanity, waiting to be corrupted.'

I say nothing.

'Meyer was the first. His coach approached me with his problems. Don't weep too hard for Meyer, Detective Carvalho. He was a big man, but he liked little girls.'

I have no reason to doubt Jaffari.

'And the others?'

'Over time, Meyer's coach recommended me to other athletes. I began to collect them. Not all of them were susceptible, but I wanted to prove that I could force normal people to do terrible things. Just like the Americans did in Abu Ghraib. Just like the Nazis at Auschwitz. This week I've pushed the button and sent them off on their missions. *Throw your javelin through the heart of the President. Kill yourself with drugs. Shoot the athlete you're secretly having an affair with.* Or wait for them to shoot you.'

He looks particularly satisfied with this last accomplishment, and his eyes glint nastily from behind Felipe's slumped torso.

'What have Carvalho and I got to do with it?' Paz asks angrily from the shadows. 'What has Felipe got to do with it?'

'This is a lifetime's work. Universities will not sanction this kind of research. There is no other way for me to prove to the world that people are so easily manipulated. Think of the implications. This will help us to understand how terrorists convince suicide bombers to blow themselves up. How armies control their soldiers. How state atrocities are performed. The world needs to see my research. And you came very close to ruining everything. Too close to my athletes.'

'Not really,' Paz says. 'They're all dead.'

Jaffari smiles again.

'So how did you do it?' I ask him. 'How did you convince them to sacrifice themselves?'

His cold eyes flick back to me.

'Simple. I made it their best option. Everyone has a weak spot. Take Paz, for example. For Paz, her weakness is her son. This is why Paz is going to shoot you. Right now. Right between the eyes. Because if she doesn't, I'll shoot little Felipe here.'

The words hang heavy in the air for a moment.

'You see, she likes you. But she likes Felipe more. Just like I said before, pressure is a button. And I just pressed it.'

CHAPTER 22

PAZ'S ANGER TURNS TO horror, but as Jaffari pushes his gun hard against her son's head, she lifts her own weapon and points it slowly towards me. Buying time, maybe. In the shadows she lifts herself to her feet and, despite everything, I'm forced to cover her with my own gun. I have spent a lifetime on some of the world's most dangerous streets. There's a reason that I'm still here. I play the game pretty simply: if someone points a gun at me, I point mine right back at them. Even if it's Paz. I watch her down the barrel. She's like a marionette, fighting against her own strings. Every move is laboured, reluctant and inevitable.

'Drop your weapon,' Jaffari tells me. 'You're spoiling all the fun. Drop it now, or I will kill the boy.'

I have no choice. I lower my gun to my side and reluctantly drop it onto the wooden floor.

'You are one twisted son of a bitch,' I tell Jaffari, as Paz walks from the shadows into the gloomy light. Her eyes are suddenly dull and lifeless, submitting to the task ahead.

'Science is everything,' Jaffari says, 'and pressure is just a button. Paz shoots you, or I shoot the boy. There's the pressure. You know she's going to do it, Carvalho. What choice does she have? She's a cog in a system, just like the soldiers at Abu Ghraib. Soon people will understand the human machine, and the people who can manipulate us into doing terrible things.'

I realise that Jaffari is no longer talking to me, but delivering a sermon to the camera. The tiny red dot is still glowing in the dark, filming over Paz's shoulder.

'You have become the exact thing you are fighting against,' I tell him. 'A perversion of your original idea. You are enjoying this power. The thrill has corrupted you. Don't you see the irony? You might as well be working in Abu Ghraib. You're an insult to your brother's memory.'

Angering Jaffari is my only chance to change the game. If I can goad him into pointing his gun at me, even for a split second, we will win. If Jaffari moves his gun just an inch away from Felipe's head, Paz will not hesitate to end this thing. However, Jaffari stays calm, and I can't get a rise out of him.

'People will understand,' he continues. 'A bit of psychology, some precise hypnosis and a little neurolinguistic programming, and someone like me can make an average person do almost anything. Even the greatest athletes in the world can have instructions embedded in their minds.'

'Kill-codes,' Paz says, staring at me over her gun.

'Well, here's the thing,' I tell Jaffari as Paz walks slowly towards me. 'I don't think you understand people at all.'

I stare straight into the psychologist's eyes, and for a brief second he looks unsettled. Then Paz steps between us, her gun trained on my head. As she moves closer with her arms stretched out, pointing her weapon at me, I can see Jaffari staring over her shoulder with the faintest trace of doubt registering across his olive features.

With good reason.

With her back turned on her tormentor, Paz's dull eyes light up. They burn with cold fury, and although I don't know what she is planning, I am certain that we're on the same side. Just like always. As she reaches me, she lets go of the butt and lets the weight of the gun rotate it around her finger.

In the distance, sirens sound and Jaffari's composure fades. It takes him about a second to realise that I never called the mobile phone on the table. I phoned for backup. Now the GPS in my phone is guiding the cavalry home. His chair scrapes on the rough wooden floor and he pushes himself to his feet, dragging Felipe with him like a shield.

'Have some pressure of your own,' I tell him, and his face contorts with rage.

I look back at Paz, who looks me in the eye and mouths, 'Don't miss.'

I reach forward and take the primed gun from my partner, her body shielding the transaction from Jaffari's view. When I have it in my hands, Paz spins to one side and I get a split-second view of Jaffari. I could aim straight for his eye, poking out an inch to the side of Felipe's head. But no matter how hard I try, the psychological pressure of avoiding Felipe will almost certainly force me wide of the mark. However, height is on my side. Rahim Jaffari is nearly six feet tall, and Felipe is a small boy. I look down and see that everything from Jaffari's knees down is completely exposed. I don't think. I just shoot twice, and splinter both of his shins.

Jaffari's legs fail and he topples backwards, his arms flailing in an attempt to regain some control over gravity. His pistol comes away from Felipe's temple and I charge towards him, smashing the gun out of his unsteady hand. I hear the metal thump onto the wooden floor and skid into the dark corner where the video camera is still recording.

Despite his mangled legs, Jaffari is strong. He has one arm snaked around Felipe's neck and, as I get in close, he punches me hard in the side of the head. For a split second the scene goes black, and then my brain reboots and I see Paz diving between the psychologist and me. She times it badly and flies head-first into another of Jaffari's swinging punches. I hear the dull thud of the impact and see Paz drop to the ground, unconscious long before her body hits the floor. I aim Paz's gun, but the wreckage of her, her son and the psychologist is strewn across the floor. I can't get a straight shot at Jaffari without the chance that I'll hit Paz or Felipe in the process. Jaffari makes the most of my hesitation, scrabbling forward and seizing my wrist with both hands. I let the gun go, and it flies off into the shadows. It's a better option that holding on and accidentally shooting Felipe.

With mother and child lying unconscious on the floor, it's just Jaffari and me. I punch him hard in the head with my free hand, connecting close to his eye and feeling him lurch backwards. He lets go of my wrist and falls back to the floor, his mangled legs pumping arterial blood across the dusty boards. In the half light it looks black, as if I've struck oil. But the slow inevitability of his death is not enough for me. My anger betrays my good sense, and I fall to the floor and grab him by the neck. I have a primal urge to squeeze the life out of him, to crush the wicked, unrepentant malice from his body until it is entirely extinguished from the world. Outside, the sirens are getting closer, but I don't want the reinforcements to arrive. I want a long moment between us, so that I see him suffer the same fate as those young, bright athletes he chose to snuff out on a whim.

It's a mistake, of course. Even as I do it, Jaffari reaches forward, gets a grip on my neck and crushes me just as hard as I am crushing him. We grapple and twist like eels in the black blood, each of us clawing our nails into the other man's neck to counteract the slickness of Jaffari's bleeding. My head feels light as he grips like steel across my windpipe. Jaffari is a dying man and it's his last spiteful hope that he can take me with him. Suddenly, as the room begins to spin, it all stops. There are two fearsome bangs and I know at once what has happened. Paz has regained consciousness and found her gun. Both shots have hit Jaffari in the forehead, just inches from my fingers, and suddenly it is only my grip around his neck that is keeping him upright. I let go and he falls back on himself, his body twisted and his head lolling unnaturally to one side.

Paz ignores her own handiwork, stepping over Jaffari to reach Felipe. She scoops up his tiny body from the floor and pulls him into an embrace. As the room settles and my hearing begins to return, it's apparent that she's sobbing. I want to reach her, but before I make it back onto my feet, I hear the tactical team thundering up the stairs and spilling out into the room all around us. And, just like that, the whole thing is over.

CHAPTER 23

A YOUNG GIRL IS staring at me from across the street as I sit outside Casas Pedro. The girl's mother follows her gaze and sees that she's staring at the fearsome black bruising around my neck – the parting gift of a dying man. The woman takes her daughter's hand and pulls her along the street, although the child glances back over her shoulder a couple of times as she goes. I don't care about the bruising. The sun is shining and I am happy. I'm eating fried cheese rolls and a fatty pork feijoada stew, and opposite me Paz is eating the same.

'Felipe is out of hospital.'

'That's good. No lasting problems?'

'He's fine. He doesn't remember any of it.'

'Well, that's good, too. Where is he?'

'With Grandma. She won't let him out of her sight.'

The TV screen in the corner of the bar is showing reruns of the Brazilian volleyball team taking the Copacabana beach by storm. Paz seems more interested in the feijoada than the sport.

'It's good,' she says. 'But how the hell have you made it to retirement, eating this every day?'

'I haven't made it yet,' I say. 'A few days left.'

Paz laughs and takes a mouthful of the stew, the juice of it coating her lips and the rich flavour adding a sparkle to her eyes. She's still chewing when her phone rings, so I pick it up for her.

'Hello?'

I can feel the colour draining from my face as I listen. Paz studies my greying features with a look of concern.

'Okay,' I say. 'We're on our way.'

Two minutes later, the pork feijoada is a distant memory and we're weaving through the traffic to make it to the Maracanã for the closing ceremony.

'I don't understand,' Paz says as she drives hard towards the stadium. She's absently patting her pockets down as she drives, and eventually I find a battered packet of cigarettes in the glove box and hand them to her. 'What's happening?'

'We made a mistake,' I tell her. 'It's not over.'

'How can it not be over? Jaffari is dead.'

She brings both hands together at the top of the wheel and taps the bottom of the cigarette packet, waiting for me to make sense of it all.

'Remember Galina Orlov? The blonde? She's been missing all day. They've just spotted her at the stadium.'

Paz looks confused.

'We discounted Galina Orlov already.'

'Yes, because we thought we were looking for a drug-dealer. But we weren't. We were looking for someone who had been programmed to do Jaffari's dirty work. She fits the bill perfectly.

She had access to all of Jaffari's clients, and she was the trigger for what happened in the favela.'

A lone cigarette flicks free from the box and Paz's practised fingers pull it free and to her lips. She glances across at me.

'How do you figure that, Carvalho?'

'Well, Jaffari manipulated people from the shadows. So what made him suddenly tempt us into the favela to find him? Why did he suddenly decide to put himself in the frame, when we were nowhere near him?'

Paz glances across at me.

'We must have been closer than we thought,' she says from the corner of her mouth. The urgency of the situation is dawning on her, and she pushes the tiny Fiat even harder.

'Exactly. Jaffari would have expected us to find the cyclist, so that wasn't what forced him to act. Besides, he'd already taken Felipe by the time we reached the Vista Chinesa. So maybe he had plans for Galina Orlov.'

'Looks that way now,' Paz agrees.

We reach the Maracanã five minutes later. Ever since we found Jaffari, I have been treated as the hero who saved the President, rather than the person who shot Tim Gilmore. The stadium manager greets us as we arrive, with the last of the latecomers struggling to get to the final spectacular.

'We found her,' he says as we push inside. He's a beanpole of a man wearing a T-shirt and chinos. He's clutching a radio and walks swiftly alongside us as we head towards the stadium communications room. 'We've picked her up on CCTV. She's on the roof.'

An explosion of sound reverberates through the concrete structure and a rhythmic pulse follows. Outside, the closing ceremony has begun.

CHAPTER 24

THERE IS NO TIME for a long briefing.

'Follow me,' the skinny stadium manager says, and we head through the rabbit warren of restricted corridors until we arrive at a service staircase.

'What's she planning?' Paz asks as we head up the concrete steps. 'Why the roof?'

'Because it's what she does. Gilmore used his javelin. Witt and Zou used their competition pistols. Orlov is a diver, so one way or another, my guess is she's planning to jump.'

'To achieve what?'

Before I can answer, I realise we're not alone. The Policia Militar SWAT team is in position at the top of the stairs, waiting for a command to go. They're headed up by the guy I put on the floor, after I shot Gilmore. He looks contrite, but not exactly pleased to see us.

'Do you know her?'

I nod.

'Galina Orlov. Russian diver. She's injured. We spoke to her at one point during our investigation into Jaffari, but there was nothing to pin on her.'

Orlov has left the door to the roof swinging open and the cool night air is blowing in. The sound of the expectant crowd rises to greet us, and the Russian is out on the far edge of the roof, a subtle silhouette against an ink-black sky. She is perfectly balanced and her palms are outstretched to meet the wind, like Christ the Redeemer on the top of Corcovado Mountain.

'She's holding a banner between her hands,' the commander of the SWAT team says, pulling night-vision goggles away from his eyes. 'It looks like a web address. I can't read exactly what it says, though.'

'What's she waiting for?' Paz asks nervously.

'She's waiting for the lights to come up.'

The commander looks at me.

'Then what?'

I can see the moment unravelling in my mind.

'Then she'll jump. She'll jump when almost everybody in the world is watching. We're directly above the burning Olympic cauldron, and my guess is that Jaffari has convinced her to aim for that.'

'What the hell reason would she have for doing that?'

'The banner,' Paz tells him. 'The website. It's probably Jaffari's research, ready for global exposure.'

I sigh. 'A message from beyond the grave.'

The commander puts his goggles back to his eyes.

'How long until the lights come up?' he growls into his radio.

'Forty seconds,' the crackled reply comes back. 'A firework spectacular, right behind where you're situated.'

'I can take her out from here,' he suggests, 'while it's still dark.'

Paz looks horrified at the suggestion, and I shake my head.

'Even if you get a clean shot, she's still going to tumble forward and into the flames.'

The commander raises an eyebrow as if to say, *What's your plan then, old-timer?*

I stand up and my knees click, and I head stiffly towards the door.

'Let me go. If I fail, you might as well shoot us both.'

I grab an earpiece from the nearest Policia Militar, and before the SWAT commander can argue, I'm past him and out onto the roof. It's made of a translucent plastic and I'm aware there's nothing beneath my feet except a hell of a drop and a mass of people. The wind almost blows me off my feet as I step away from the shelter of the stairwell. My mouth instantly dries, but I keep walking, closer and closer to the athlete on the edge. I remember Steve Lewis, and how I talked him back from the brink. Somehow this feels very different. I'm on edge, and I jump as my earpiece crackles into life.

'We've checked out the web address,' a female voice says. 'You're right, it's psychological research of some kind. We're trying to get it shut down right now.'

Then the voice disappears, and I'm back on my own on the roof.

'Fifteen seconds, Rafael.'

It's Paz.

I take a breath. I have one shot at this. One sentence. *Focus.*

'Galina?'

My voice echoes out into the dark sky, and Orlov turns round. She looks as if she's in a trance, and I think about what Jaffari has done to her. How he must have chosen her because she was susceptible to his programming. And I wonder if I can use that suggestibility to save her life. It's my only hope. It's *her* only hope.

Paz crackles in my ear: 'Five seconds.'

I stand five yards from Orlov, and I make no attempt to move towards her. It would only push her over the edge. Her blonde hair is whipping across her face in the wind, but I can see in her eyes that I've engaged her. She's listening to me. I spread my arms wide to her, mirroring her Christ-pose.

'Change of plan,' I say calmly and authoritatively. 'Don't think about it. Just come to me.'

Galina Orlov's split second of indecision feels like a lifetime. Then suddenly she blazes white, as a thousand fireworks set the sky alight. Below us, fierce white stage lighting burns through the opaque plastic roof. We are the centre of the world's attention. Orlov takes all of this as some kind of sign, and does exactly what I have told her to do. I can feel the SWAT team's weapons trained on her as she walks slowly into my arms, and I wrap them around her so that she is completely safe. Below, the crowd go wild, imagining that the whole scene on the roof is an orchestrated part of the show.

I look across at Paz and our eyes lock. In the fierce light, I can see tears begin to spill from her eyes – not for Galina Orlov, but for me. Because Paz knows what I know: this is the end. The end of a lifetime of work, and the last moment in a case that we have won. We saved the ones we could, and that's enough for me. Paz nods, and braves a smile. I feel Orlov slacken in my arms, as if she has finally understood the danger she was in. I hold her up and begin to guide her back to the stairwell, where the SWAT team is hanging out of the door, beckoning us towards them.

For the first time, a wave of vertigo crashes over me as the wind picks up again, whipping something away from Orlov's slack hand. It's the banner, the thin white strip of paper with Jaffari's web address written boldly across it. The one that was supposed to be seen by every TV station in the world. Instead, it snakes across the translucent plastic roof and falls like ticker tape, burning up as it reaches the Olympic flame far below.

CHAPTER 25

THE CELEBRATIONS CONTINUE AROUND the stadium as I climb back through the access door and into the stairwell, with Galina Orlov clinging to me like a child.

'What was I doing?'

'Just what you'd been told,' I say, as the SWAT team peels her away from me and guides her down the concrete stairs to safety. Only the commander remains, but before he says anything, Paz bear-hugs me and slaps me hard on the back.

'You're a brave guy, Carvalho,' she tells me. 'Christ knows, I'm going to miss you when you're gone.'

I close the rooftop door, sliding a heavy bolt into place behind me. *When I'm gone.* Despite my aching bones, I know I'm going to miss moments like this. As I turn, Paz's phone rings, and the SWAT commander takes his chance to grab my hand. His grip is firm and honest.

'Look after Galina Orlov,' I tell him. 'She's been through a lot.'

'Sure,' he says. 'Look after yourself as well.'

He turns to leave, but only gets a couple of steps before stopping and heading back to me.

'Listen,' he says. 'I was out of order when we first met. You're a hell of a brave guy, and I wish I'd shown you a bit more respect.'

'No, you were right. I'm an old-timer. But so will you be, one day. And then you'll realise that life's not about the rank on your shoulders, it's about what's in here.'

I push my fist onto his chest, the same place he pushed me when we first met. He doesn't yield any more than I did.

'Well, good luck, *old-timer*,' he says with an open smile.

I wish him the same, as he heads down to join his unit. Beside me, Paz is cradling her phone under her chin and looking like a scolded child.

'It's Juliana. She's just seen you on TV. She wants to know what you're doing on the roof?'

'Tell her I'm coming down.'

Whatever Juliana says to Paz, it makes her smile.

'She says she's not happy.'

'Tell her I promise I won't do it again.'

The promise hangs in the air, because we both know it's true. I am days away from the end. In the quiet stairwell, we can hear the crowd cheering behind the bolted door, and I suddenly feel like the party is a million miles away.

'What's the world record for getting from the Maracanã to Casas Pedro?'

Paz smiles a Mona Lisa smile.

'You fancy a cold beer, Detective Carvalho?'

For a moment, I think of the athletes we saved, and the athletes we lost, and the justice we gave them in the Vila Cruzeiro favela.

'A beer sounds like a good plan, Detective Paz. Let's go and raise a glass.'

A man plunges to his death from the roof of a Manhattan hotel. It looks like a suicide – but why does the victim have someone else's fingerprints?

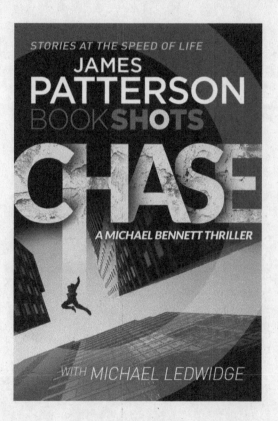

Read on for an extract

AT THE END of the dark, crowded bar, a man in black twirled an e-cigarette through his fingers and over his thumb like a little baton, again and again as he watched and waited.

It was an aggravating, fidgety habit, he knew. But when he was anxious, it was harder to resist than smoking the damn thing.

The bar was in a hip industrial-chic hotel on 67th and Broadway called Index House, with a cutting-edge meets Roaring Twenties vibe. Charging stations blended into a décor of exposed brick and tufted chairs. With his downtown black silk suit and dark *GQ* looks, the man belonged there.

He deftly flipped the cigarette into his inside jacket pocket as the bartender finally approached with his drink. It was a Zombie, four or five different rums and some cognac with a splash of pineapple and mango juice. One of the rums was 151-proof, and flammable. He'd seen drinks lit on fire many times over the last seven years, in many places, from Jamaica to Jakarta.

Too damn many, he thought.

"So are you a *Walking Dead* fanatic, or do you just like the demon rum?" the doe-eyed bartender asked, over the crowd murmur and slow jazz piano playing from the lobby.

There were two bartenders, a guy and a girl, but he had ordered from the guy.

"*Entschuldigen Sie?*" he said, staring at her like he'd just stepped off a flying saucer. It meant "excuse me" in German. The one and only phrase he'd picked up in three useless months in Munich four years ago.

That did the trick. She went away with his two twenties, and quick. Lovely as she was, he didn't need any distractions. Not now. He began rubbing his thighs nervously as he scanned the hotel lobby. He looked out at the dark of Broadway through the plate glass behind him, a clear moonless October evening in New York, bright lights twinkling.

At this critical juncture, he needed to stay on his damn toes.

Where the hell is this guy? he thought, taking out his phone to check his messages. It was 9:25. Almost a half hour late and still no call. Did this joker's phone die? He just wasn't coming? No way to know. Great. He'd just sit here on his ass some more.

He placed his phone on the zinc bar top and reached for the drink. Then he stopped himself and instead took out the e-cigarette again. Back and forth, and back and forth, over and through his fingers faster and faster, he twirled the metal cigarette until it was just a black blur across his knuckles.

IN THE CROWDED library off the hotel bar, Devine sat listening to the boss man on the phone.

"What's Pretty Boy doing now?"

"Nothing," Devine said. "Just sitting at the bar, playing with a pen or something. Got himself a tropical drink. He's looking a little melancholy. And nervous."

"That right?" the boss said.

Devine, who was from Tennessee, loved the boss's hard-ass southern voice, the power in it. It reminded him of a backwoods Baptist minister, perpetually on the verge of going all fire-and-brimstone on his congregation.

"Well, he's going to be singing the blues all right. You just make sure you don't join him for a few. He slips away again, it's your ass."

Devine winced. He didn't take criticism well. Especially from one of the few people he respected.

"So, plan is still in place?" Devine said. "Hit him when he goes back to his room?"

"Yes, Devine. You remembered from five minutes ago. Bravo," said the boss. "But if a chance comes up right there in the bar, if you can be discreet, you take it. That's why I sent you in instead of Toporski. You know how to improvise."

Devine shook his head as the boss hung up. He'd never heard the man so tense, so—dare he say it—nervous. Pretty Boy had him rattled. Had them all rattled.

That's why they were up in New York now, all of them. There was a team a short block west in front of a gym on 67th and Amsterdam, and another outside the hotel.

They had Pretty Boy boxed in once and for all.

"El Jefe still got his boxers in a wad, eh?" said Therkelson.

"Yep," Devine said as he glanced over at the blond, middle linebacker–sized Therkelson. His big iron Swede thumbs were flying on his Galaxy, playing some game. "You know, Therk, you got a real funny way of conducting surveillance with your face in that phone."

"Ah," Therkelson said, not even glancing up. "You got it covered. I'm the muscle here in our little partnership, Timmy. Be wrong not to let you do anything. I want to make sure a little guy like you feels like you're contributing."

DEVINE MUNCHED A handful of complimentary jalapeño peanuts as he kept his eyes trained on the target.

He didn't know how they'd tracked Pretty Boy down. A few of the guys were saying the boss man had an old friend in the NSA, which seemed valid. With access to phone and credit card tracking, you could pinpoint any old Tom, Dick, or Harry in the civilized part of the planet in half an hour.

And *what* Pretty Boy was doing, they didn't know that, either. All they knew was that it wasn't part of the playbook. He'd bugged out for a little R&R for the long weekend like the rest of them, but then come Tuesday, he didn't show up. No word.

That was a week ago. Now they'd finally run him down, here in New York in this fancy Pajama Boy gin mill, of all places.

Devine watched as the hot bartender tossed Pretty Boy another interested glance. *Had a woman, even an ugly one, ever looked at him like that?* he thought. No. Not even when he gave them the money first. The bitter inequities of the world.

Yeah, Devine thought, nodding as he looked at Pretty Boy. He was going to enjoy this little piece of work.

It was about three minutes later when Pretty Boy put down his empty glass and stood up. He was heading toward the can. Devine had been monitoring it. There was no one in there.

Welcome to an evening at the improv, Devine thought as he suddenly slapped the phone into Therkelson's lap.

"C'mon," he said, already moving as he watched Pretty Boy push open the restroom door.

He sent Therkelson in by himself while he watched the hall to keep out any civilians. He heard some scuffling behind the door, a muffled grunt. Therkelson knew his orders. Neutralize him, then do a strip search if necessary.

He waited a full minute, checking his stainless steel Rolex, and then another.

What the hell was taking him so long? Devine thought.

He couldn't take it anymore. He pushed open the door.

And came face to face with the shocking and unthinkable.

Therkelson, the incredible Therk himself, was lying unmoving, facedown on the white tile.

As if that weren't enough, as Devine stood there still gaping in wide wonder, one of the stall doors slammed open and cracked him right in the forehead.

An instant later came a searing pain in his neck as Pretty Boy hit him with Therkelson's stun gun for a buzzing moment. Devine threw up jalapeño peanuts all over himself when Pretty

Boy savagely kneed him in the balls. Several times, lightning-quick, like a Thai boxer.

Before he knew it, Devine was down next to Therkelson on his hands and knees like a baby, seeing stars in the tile work. Pretty Boy leapt him like a track hurdle and exited.

Palming himself up from his own vomit a few dazed and throbbing minutes later, Devine shook his head as he fished out his phone.

Here we go again, he thought as he dialed the boss man.

THE MAN IN black was a serious runner. He ran seventy miles a week on a strict plan. He did tempo runs and speed training. He didn't just run 5Ks, he usually won them.

But he was gasping like a day-one Biggest Loser and had sweated clean through the back of his suit jacket by the time he came up the sixteen flights of steps and burst from the stairwell door out onto the hotel's roof deck.

He scanned the deck. Dark blue-black sky and cold air. Rattan couches under string lights. A gas fire pit turned off now. No people. No team. They weren't up here. At least not yet.

He thought he could find a way out the back of the hotel, but there was only the stairwell. There was no way he could have gone out the front. If Devine and Therkelson were here, they were all here, strung out in a perimeter.

He was in a slipknot now, which was tightening as he stood there.

Beyond the fire pit, there was an enclosed rooftop bar with a Reserved sign on a stand in front of its French doors. Through the glass, he could see guests and wait staff and tables set with flowers and white linens. A DJ in a tuxedo shirt bent by a turntable, and then there was a sudden blast of swinging trumpets and Sinatra singing "Come Dance with Me."

Clueless civilians. No help in that direction. No time to even ask.

He went to the roof's edge and looked down on Broadway. Sixteen stories down. Two lanes of moving traffic. Lights of Lincoln Center. Some people on the sidewalk. No way to tell the good guys from the bad guys.

He rushed along the roof deck, skirting the building's perimeter to 67th Street, looking for a fire escape. At the northeastern edge of the building down 67th, he was hoping for another building he could escape onto, but there was nothing except a huge empty dirt lot with a bunch of construction equipment.

He'd come along the southeastern back corner of the hotel when he finally saw his out.

Behind the hotel was an old building under renovation. They were doing brickwork and had an outside scaffold set up, a cruciform track running from roof to ground with a movable scaffold forming the horizontal part of the cross. The right-hand end of the scaffold was about fifteen feet away from where he was standing, and about a floor and a half below the level of the hotel roof.

He looked behind him at the path he'd just come down. If he went back to the other edge of the hotel by 67th, ran full-out and got a little height as he leapt off the top of the waist-high wall, he could do it. He could long jump it.

Don't think. Don't look down. Just do it.

He made it to the other end of the roof deck and had turned back for his running start when Therkelson came out of the shadow on his right and grabbed him.

Forgetting his knife, the dark-haired man scrambled with animal panic to break the bigger, stronger man's iron grip. He bashed the big son of a bitch in his mouth with the heel of his right hand, trying to get a thumb in his eye with his left.

But Therkelson didn't let go.

Gripping the struggling dark-haired man by his lapels, Therkelson lifted him up off his feet and, without preamble, easily and silently threw him hard off the side of the building.

In that first terrible instant out in the black space and open cold air, the dark-haired man saw the city around him, like an upside-down I♥NY postcard snapshot. Window lights and water towers and the setbacks on the apartment buildings.

Then he was spinning and falling, the cold air rushing and ripping in his eyes and face.

No, no, no! Can't, can't! Not now! he thought over the blasting of the air and his heart, as he free-fell faster and faster through the cold and black—down, down, down.

JAMES PATTERSON
BOOKSHOTS
OUT THIS MONTH

CHASE: A MICHAEL BENNETT THRILLER

A man falls to his death in an apparent accident. But why does he have the fingerprints of another man who is already dead? Detective Michael Bennett is on the case.

LET'S PLAY MAKE-BELIEVE

Christy and Marty just met, and it's love at first sight. Or is it? One of them is playing a dangerous game – and only one will survive.

DEAD HEAT

Detective Carvalho is investigating the disappearance of a key athlete on the day of the opening ceremony of the 2016 Olympic Games. The case is about to take a deadly turn …

THE McCULLAGH INN IN MAINE

Chelsea O'Kane escapes to Maine to build a new life – until she runs into her old flame Jeremy Holland …

TRIPLE THREAT

Three pulse-pounding stories in one book! *Cross Kill*, *Zoo 2* and *The Pretender*.

THE PRETENDER (ebook only)

Logan Bishop is a thief living off a stash of stolen diamonds. But when his murderous ex-partner tracks him down, Logan could lose it all …

JAMES PATTERSON
BOOK**SHOTS**
COMING SOON

113 MINUTES

Molly Rourke's son has been murdered ... and she knows who's responsible. Now she's taking the law into her own hands.

THE VERDICT

A billionaire businessman is on trial for violently attacking a woman in her bed. No one is prepared for the terrifying consequences of the verdict.

THE MATING SEASON

Sophie Castle has been given the opportunity of a lifetime: her own wildlife documentary. But her cameraman, Rigg Greensman, is unmotivated ... and drop dead gorgeous.

BOOKSHOTS

STORIES AT THE SPEED OF LIFE

www.bookshots.com

ALSO BY JAMES PATTERSON

ALEX CROSS NOVELS

Along Came a Spider

Kiss the Girls

Jack and Jill

Cat and Mouse

Pop Goes the Weasel

Roses are Red

Violets are Blue

Four Blind Mice

The Big Bad Wolf

London Bridges

Mary, Mary

Cross

Double Cross

Cross Country

Alex Cross's Trial (*with Richard DiLallo*)

I, Alex Cross

Cross Fire

Kill Alex Cross

Merry Christmas, Alex Cross

Alex Cross, Run

Cross My Heart

Hope to Die

Cross Justice

THE WOMEN'S MURDER CLUB SERIES

1st to Die

2nd Chance (*with Andrew Gross*)

3rd Degree (*with Andrew Gross*)

4th of July (*with Maxine Paetro*)

The 5th Horseman (*with Maxine Paetro*)

The 6th Target (*with Maxine Paetro*)

7th Heaven (*with Maxine Paetro*)

8th Confession (*with Maxine Paetro*)

9th Judgement (*with Maxine Paetro*)

10th Anniversary (*with Maxine Paetro*)

11th Hour (*with Maxine Paetro*)

12th of Never (*with Maxine Paetro*)

Unlucky 13 (*with Maxine Paetro*)

14th Deadly Sin (*with Maxine Paetro*)

15th Affair (*with Maxine Paetro*)

DETECTIVE MICHAEL BENNETT SERIES

Step on a Crack (*with Michael Ledwidge*)

Run for Your Life (*with Michael Ledwidge*)

Worst Case (*with Michael Ledwidge*)

Tick Tock (*with Michael Ledwidge*)

I, Michael Bennett (*with Michael Ledwidge*)

Gone (*with Michael Ledwidge*)

Burn (*with Michael Ledwidge*)

Alert (*with Michael Ledwidge*)

Bullseye (*with Michael Ledwidge*)

PRIVATE NOVELS

Private (*with Maxine Paetro*)

Private London (*with Mark Pearson*)

Private Games (*with Mark Sullivan*)

Private: No. 1 Suspect (*with Maxine Paetro*)

Private Berlin (*with Mark Sullivan*)

Private Down Under (*with Michael White*)

Private L.A. (*with Mark Sullivan*)

Private India (*with Ashwin Sanghi*)

Private Vegas (*with Maxine Paetro*)

Private Sydney (*with Kathryn Fox*)

Private Paris (*with Mark Sullivan*)

The Games (*with Mark Sullivan*)

NYPD RED SERIES

NYPD Red (*with Marshall Karp*)

NYPD Red 2 (*with Marshall Karp*)

NYPD Red 3 (*with Marshall Karp*)

NYPD Red 4 (*with Marshall Karp*)

STAND-ALONE THRILLERS

Sail (*with Howard Roughan*)

Swimsuit (*with Maxine Paetro*)

Don't Blink (*with Howard Roughan*)

Postcard Killers (*with Liza Marklund*)

Toys (*with Neil McMahon*)

Now You See Her (*with Michael Ledwidge*)

Kill Me If You Can (*with Marshall Karp*)

Guilty Wives (*with David Ellis*)

Zoo (*with Michael Ledwidge*)

Second Honeymoon (*with Howard Roughan*)

Mistress (*with David Ellis*)

Invisible (*with David Ellis*)

The Thomas Berryman Number

Truth or Die (*with Howard Roughan*)

Murder House (*with David Ellis*)

NON-FICTION

Torn Apart (*with Hal and Cory Friedman*)

The Murder of King Tut (*with Martin Dugard*)

ROMANCE

Sundays at Tiffany's (*with Gabrielle Charbonnet*)

The Christmas Wedding (*with Richard DiLallo*)

First Love (*with Emily Raymond*)

OTHER TITLES

Miracle at Augusta (*with Peter de Jonge*)

BOOKSHOTS

Black & Blue (*with Candice Fox*)

Break Point (*with Lee Stone*)

Cross Kill

Private Royals (*with Rees Jones*)

The Hostage (*with Robert Gold*)

Zoo 2 (*with Max DiLallo*)

Heist (*with Rees Jones*)

Hunted (*with Andrew Holmes*)

Airport: Code Red (*with Michael White*)

The Trial (*with Maxine Paetro*)

Little Black Dress (*with Emily Raymond*)